Harry and Hortense
at Hormone
High

Also by Paul Zindel

Confessions of a Teenage Baboon
The Effect of Gamma Rays on Man-in-the-Moon Marigolds
  (a play)
The Girl Who Wanted a Boy
I Love My Mother
  (a picture book, illustrated by John Melo)
I Never Loved Your Mind
Let Me Hear You Whisper
  (a play, illustrated by Stephen Gammell)
My Darling, My Hamburger
Pardon Me, You're Stepping On My Eyeball!
The Pigman
The Pigman's Legacy
A Star For the Latecomer
  (with Bonnie Zindel)
To Take a Dare
  (with Crescent Dragonwagon)
The Undertaker's Gone Bananas

Harry and Hortense at Hormone High

Paul Zindel

Harper & Row, Publishers

1 2 3 4 5 6 7 8 9 10
First Edition

Library of Congress Cataloging in Publication Data
Zindel, Paul.
    Harry and Hortense at Hormone High.

    "A Charlotte Zolotow book."
    Summary: Two teenagers think they may have found a
hero in a schizophrenic boy who thinks he is Icarus.
    [1. Mentally ill—Fiction.   2. Friendship—Fiction.
3. High schools—Fiction.   4. Schools—Fiction]   I. Title.
PZ7.Z647Har   1984   [Fic]   82-47697
ISBN 0-06-026864-6
ISBN 0-06-026869-7 (lib. bdg.)

Dedicated to a couple of
    great kids called David and Lizabeth . . .
To Bonnie, the goddess . . .
And to Miss Marilyn Marlow, the teacher in charge
    of the stockroom who let us borrow Board of Ed
        typewriter paper and gave us amulets against
            the Dragon Forces . . .
And to Laura . . .
And Gina,
And Bill,
And Joan,
And Jeannette,
And
To Charlotte,
    of course!

Harry and Hortense at Hormone High

1

Hortense and I were so depressed last term, we used to get together every Saturday night to split a can of diet Pepsi Free and talk about how mean most of the kids and teachers were to each other in our high school. But that was all before we met Jason Rohr, the most dynamic and exciting teenage schizophrenic we've ever known.

Jason Rohr was a boy who changed our lives. He's gone now, but I feel it's my duty to write down all that he taught us so that in case you're sitting in a classroom thinking your life, zodiac guide, parents, peers, and planet Earth are all a big sad crock—well, that's why we want you to know about Jason, because what he told us might help. You might as well know right now that Jason Rohr died on May 15 of this year. There's no point in saving that up like some kind of last-minute Brian De Palma shock ending or something. Jason Rohr died near our high school, and he

3

was the third one to die this year. The first one was Johnnie Frank, who fell asleep drunk while smoking a Benson and Hedges 100-centimeter cigarette and went up in flames. The second was David Johnson, who was found deceased floating in a Toys R Us plastic swimming pool in Port Richmond, and the cops said he was just a simple O.D.

What you also need to know up front is that our school is so bonkers that even the teachers can't stand it, which is why during the course of this exposé I am writing I have to call it Hormone High. If we called it by its real name, everyone would know exactly which teenage loony bin it is, and the Board of Education would probably come after us and knock us off by making us eat three consecutive monosodium glutamate Mongolian chop sueys in the school cafeteria.

At Hormone High a lot of the kids wear status perfumes and have brand names written on their buns. And that's just the football team. What's worse, three kids in our honor society swear they saw Mr. Rickenbacker, our shop teacher, on the Staten Island ferry dressed as Olivia Newton-John like she looks at the *end* of *Grease*. They say they chased him up to the second deck, past the snack bar, but somehow he got away.

All these tidbits of data are just my way of letting you know that at my high school we don't have very many heroes or heroines. We've got weirdos. They do things like steal Walkmans from blind people, watch *Roadrunner* cartoons all Saturday mornings, and throw kiwi fruit at the movie screens of our local Cinema I, II, III, and IV. I sometimes wonder how they feel when they look at themselves in a mirror, or see a beautiful sunset.

I took a poll once with Hortense of the teachers and students in our school, and we decided 83% wished they

4

were somewhere else. Miss Ritson, an accounting teacher, told us she wished she was a musical comedy star, and once she sang in our assembly. She had a really beautiful voice, but the kids booed. Old Mr. Harrison, the math teacher, only went into teaching to avoid the World War II draft. Joey Masterson, a nice kid in our biology class, wished he could stay home all day watching reruns of *The Attack of the Killer Computer Chips*. Helen Fitzbugh, a cheerleader, really wanted to join a convent because she said nuns are disappearing. Miss Gale, our current events teacher, wished she was on a sabbatical so she could complete a best-seller she was writing called *Five Famous Men Who Were Full-Time or Part-Time Virgins*—which she said included Sir Isaac Newton, George Bernard Shaw, and Adolf Hitler. And Mrs. Hoffmann, the cooking teacher, once let Hortense and me read a short story she wrote about a poodle who falls in love with a Detroit taxicab driver. It brought tears to Hortense's eyes.

Nobody's really doing what they want to at Hormone High. Mrs. Reilland is the clerk at the front office and has to take care of latecomers and issue them passes. A lot of the kids bring her in an apple because they trust her. They hollow out the apple and shove their stash of grass in the middle of it and tell Mrs. Reilland to keep the apple until school's over. Mrs. Reilland told Hortense and me that there is no way to save the school system anymore. That it's gone too far over the edge, and something drastic has to happen soon. Or somebody great and brave has to come along to change it.

She keeps a sign over her desk that says:

MARIA MONTESSORI TAUT ME TO RITE
AT AGE TOO!!!!!!!!!!!!!!!!

Now I never liked school, even from the second grade when the teachers all thought I had dyslexia because I was reading too slowly. Dyslexia is when they think you see things backward, but in my case it was only the 321-pound Hungarian school psychologist who was backward. My mother used to push me into the best private schools, but then my family nearly went broke when my father went through male menopause and lost a lot of his advertising accounts at Blitzman and Blitzman, Inc., where he works. Hortense diagnosed him as having an "authenticity" crisis, which is what happens to a lot of fathers who turn forty and suddenly see they've been trapped into a whole mess of baloney. If we were rich I'd probably still be in that fancy private school, but now I go to Hormone High, which is as public as you can get.

In the beginning I tried to become an enthusiastic part of the Hormone High student body, but let me tell you, having a name like Harry Hickey is not the best passport to popularity. Why my parents called me Harry I can't say. And why they didn't change their name from Hickey I will never know. My parents don't know what it's like nowadays, when all the kids at school think my last name means either a hick from the sticks or a love bite. And Harry is such an old-fashioned name. They probably meant well, but why couldn't they have called me Rocky or Biff? I could have turned into a complete nerd if my father hadn't told me about an ex-President of the United States, Give-'em-Hell Harry Truman. I decided *that* would be my motto. For example, my freshman English teacher told me I *had* to enjoy Shakespeare and I told her Shakespeare was a bore. She screamed at me in front of the whole class that EVERY-BODY loved Shakespeare, and I asked the class if she was right and the whole class screamed back NO! So I got dragged to Dean Niboff's office, where I had to show them a quote from Samuel Pepys, who said in 1687 that he found Shakespeare a bore, too. And I told them if they didn't want to trust a famous English critic, they could read what the American scholar Frances Trollope said to some woman in 1850: "Shakespeare, Madam, is obscene, and, thank God, we are sufficiently advanced to have found it out!" So you see, if anybody gives *me* hell, I give it right back to them.

I'm rather basically good-looking, but not in the usual sense. I'm tall, which doesn't really mean anything since a lot of famous historical people were dwarfs and they did O.K. Hortense says my face makes me look like a "charming, devilish, darling, big elf." She says I've got "gold-green" eyes, and my mouth is always open which makes me look like I'm constantly ready for a kiss. She also says I have a lot of strength and I'm very brave, and that she's sure that's what Jason Rohr saw in me, too. I guess I'm the kind of kid who will try anything once. We were at a party one weekend, and some kid told me he had some Honolulu mushrooms and would I like a bite, and I said yes. Well, after five minutes I thought the carpet in the living room was chasing me, and Hortense had to hold me down until the effect of the mushrooms wore off.

The other thing you're going to find out about me is that I like quotes, so every once in a while I'll remember something somebody famous said, and I'll write it down because I think good writers have to do that—and that's exactly what my dream in life is—to be a *good* writer. I think I have to be grateful and give credit to all the fine writers and smart people who have been on the earth before me.

On days when I feel I'm not brave enough or that I'm never going to be as daring as Jason Rohr, I remember something Will Rogers said: "We can't all be heroes, because someone has to sit on the curb and applaud as they go by." Jason Rohr was someone we finally learned to clap for!

But that's sort of starting to get into some things that involve Hortense, too.

2

Now if I don't like *my* name, you can imagine how Hortense feels about being called Hortense. But she's one of the most fascinating and striking girls I've ever known. She's about five foot two, with very black straight hair that she wears in bangs. She's very distinctive and told me her hairstyle is called the China doll style. And she has a very slightly cute nose, about three freckles, and wears makeup that makes her eyes look like Elizabeth Taylor's as Cleopatra.

Hortense and I are very different because she comes from a very family-oriented background. Her grandparents and aunts and uncles and her mother and father are very close to each other. They all visit each other whenever they feel like it. Everyone in her family takes time to talk to each other, and there's always time to sit down and have a cup of coffee or a glass of milk or even fresh-made waffles. In my family everybody loves each other, but we don't often show it—and you're lucky if you can even find a putrefying carton of Liquid Quiche or a stale chicken leg for an afternoon snack. My folks don't really want me to have anybody over, and that makes me feel pretty bad sometimes, but I know it's mainly because they have some personal problems of their own right now. I know they still love me.

Hortense and I have known each other since the seventh grade, when Miss Stillwell made us draw a colored-chalk drawing of Madame Curie Discovering Radium on the blackboard. And it just seemed from then on Hortense and I have always understood each other. Then last November we sort of looked into each other's eyes one day over a chocolate chip cookie—and we fell in love. I mean we became very, very close. You also don't have to know *how* close we became, because our romance isn't the bigtime in this book. There are a lot more important things here than unbridled passion and lust in the video arcade palaces. This story is so important we want senators to read it, too. Jason Rohr was a boy concerned with the highest ideals on earth, not with shenanigans behind the local Bonerama.

I'm writing this book in the office of the *Bird's Eye Gazette*—which is the official newspaper of Hormone High. Sometimes Hortense sits next to me making sure the story's mainly like we both remember it. The faculty advisor is Mr. Olsen, who's the nicest old man you ever knew in your life. He's not so good as a classroom teacher now, because he's gotten a little senile, and they're going to retire him soon, but all of us kids on the *Bird's Eye* think he's terrific. He used to be famous and work at *The New York Times* doing stories about the first H-bomb and famous medicines derived from moldy bread. Some of the kids from the staff of the *Bird's Eye* have gone on to literary careers in places like Indians' Bluff, Idaho, and one's in charge of a teletype machine in a Parsippany, New Jersey radio station, an NBC affiliate. Anyway, the *Bird's Eye Gazette* office in Room 317 is really a great place to hang out, especially if you have a headache or want to cut a class. Hortense and I are the exclusive theater critics for the *Bird's Eye*. We got the position because nobody else at Hormone High was the least bit interested. Nobody even *reads* our column except to see if their names are in it. We print all students' names in extra *heavy* black. Last year we reviewed *Hamlet, Bye, Bye, Birdie, Oedipus the King*, and *Li'l Abner*. This year so far we've done things like *An Enemy of the People* and *Little Mary Sunshine*. Hortense and I learned to pad the reviews with a lot of names. There's usually only about thirty-five kids who show up to see Ibsen and one thousand eight hundred for *Bye, Bye, Birdie*. We write things in our reviews like: "**Joey Martin** was multifaceted in the lead, and **Lurie Bonza, Jackie Carton, B. J. Sussman**, and **Bob Wallha** were in the audience applauding Hamlet's melancholy." What we don't mention is that Lurie, Jackie, B. J., and Bobo also were stoned out of their minds and had brought copies of *Hamlet* so they could shout out Hamlet's lines from the audience before he said them onstage just like they do at *The Rocky Horror Picture Show*. The best we ever did was somehow manage to get eighty-seven names into a review of a play that had only five characters. That's been the secret of our entire journalistic success.

Hortense isn't all that interested in journalism as a career. She mainly expects to grow up and be a world-famous psychiatrist. She says she knows that she'll be treating the hordes of mentally ill. Even now kids come to her to help solve their problems. She's read almost everything written

11

by Freud, Jung, and some analyst called Harry Stack Sullivan. She's not a *brain* or anything like that, but she just happens to have a sixth sense about what's really bothering you.

She says only about 25% of the kids and staff at our school are normal. What she means is that there are some kids who *like* going to school, doing their homework, and learning. They enjoy themselves. And the normal teachers are the ones who obviously love their jobs, who like teaching kids, and who aren't panting to punch out early.

Hortense keeps a journal, and I think we should share a little of the gossip she's recorded so you'll understand better the kind of school Jason Rohr had to deal with when he got to Hormone High. *Gossip Facts from Hormone High*: 1. James Rebback, 15, and Helen Day, 14, were brought into the Dean's office for sensuous activities across the street from the school on a lady's lawn. They said the school had no right messing with them because they weren't on school grounds. 2. Mrs. Weider, 28, made love with Jack Cabsiewski, 17, following one of the meetings of the bowling club at Bowl City. Mrs. Weider said it was really Jack Cabsiewski who seduced her, which everyone knows is true, but that's life. Mrs. Weider now teaches Yiddish as a second language in Barcelona, Spain. 3. Louise Cleaver, 14, accused Miss Van der Knapp in biology of being a racist and beat Miss Van der Knapp all the way to the Principal's office with a blackboard eraser. 4. Mary Anne Slowty comes to school every Friday carrying her own pillow because she stays over at her boyfriend's house on weekends. She says she can't sleep on *his* pillow because it's too hard. 5. Rosemary Fleish brought statutory rape charges against Jack Martin even though they've been get-

12

ting physical for five years. Rosemary got jealous because Jack started dating Jessie Lynn McPherson.

I can understand that. Actually, I was a bit jealous when Hortense first started being friendly with Jason—well, more than just a bit. I guess I'm still jealous in a way because she still thinks about Jason a lot. So do I, but that's different. Of course, Jason was really great, but as Hortense would say, I was "full of ambivalence" about him from the word go.

3

Right here I'd better show you the note Hortense and I saw tacked up about a month ago on the bulletin board near our school's main entrance. By the time she and I got to the bulletin board, there were already about twenty other kids gathered around laughing at it. Anyway, this is what it said:

ATTENTION ALL STUDENTS!!!

I am posting this note on the main bulletin board because I want you to know that you're not all as destructive and corrupt as you act. I know you don't really mean it when you smash eggs on windshields, spray paint curse words on the walls—and throw wads of wet toilet paper up so they'll stick on the ceilings.

I am here now and will help fix everything up. Watch

for future bulletins. *Read them before the Evil Forces of Doom or the Dean rips them down.*

ICARUS, a god

Hortense and I read it, and figured it was just one more joke some kid decided to tack up, but it did sound a little more creative than most Hormone High gags—and the fact that "god" was not capitalized seemed an interesting touch. But like everybody else we just forgot about it and went on to class. By third period we did notice the letter had been ripped down.

About a week after that, Hortense and I got to school a little late one morning, and there was a big crowd around the bulletin board again reading and jeering. Another letter had been tacked up. This one said:

ATTENTION! ATTENTION STUDENTS and TEACHERS!!! I am very sad and in great despair. I noticed last week that only twenty-three parents and three teachers showed up for the PTA meeting. The Principal and Dean didn't even go. Nobody cares anymore at our school.

I also noticed there were no guards at four of the street exits. Several agents of the devil were able to just walk in off the street and steal school supplies and a typewriter. But don't give up hope. Watch for more of my bulletins. And lift thy sights more to the Heavens.

ICARUS, a god

Hortense and I had barely finished reading the letter when Dean Niboff came out of his office and down the hall to rip the thing off the bulletin board himself. Everybody split, but this time Hortense and I were a little more curious about *who* was writing the notes.

The first time we ever saw Jason was on the evening of April 22 at the school. Hortense and I were there to review a production of *South Pacific* by the Hormone High drama club. It was scheduled to start at eight P.M. in the auditorium. As usual, none of the kids in it could dance or sing. At intermission both Hortense and I noticed this boy when we were buying Dr Peppers in the lobby. The boy was standing about forty feet away near the hot-pretzel line, and we saw him looking at us. Then he went over to a side exit and began slipping pieces of his pretzel to a huge black dog just outside. I want to try to be absolutely honest about everything I write about Jason, but it's going to be hard. What happened to us all has still left me a little shaky, and I have to keep a cover on some of my feelings. Hortense with her constant drive for confession won't let me skip much, though.

Anyway, suddenly there was this mysterious-looking boy, with his big black dog sitting outside on the entrance steps. We had never seen him before. He was just standing there staring at us and feeding his pet. He looked sixteen, six feet tall, and very dynamic, as though he was a star on a major soap opera. Hortense's mouth dropped open at the sight of him. In fact, I suppose you could say Hortense and I were both struck by his aura, but we both made believe we weren't. We just chatted nervously, but we knew all along this boy was dissecting us with his eyes. At one point he flashed us a little smile, and for a moment I thought

16

Hortense was going to say *hello* to him all the way across the lobby. Finally Hortense and I had to look away from the boy and dog as though to break an electrical current, and when we looked back, the two of them were gone.

"Did you know that kid?" was all Hortense asked me.

"*Who?*" I asked.

"Oh, nobody."

Then the lights flashed for us to go back for the second act of *South Pacific*, which was the part where Rocky Funicelli, the captain of the football team, portrayed Honey Bun wearing a grass skirt and two half coconuts for boobs— the cultural climax of the evening. There's no way to exactly explain that I knew an Adventure had already started for Hortense and me. Hortense and I had had a lot of adventures, but this was something strange and new. I knew we hadn't seen the last of that boy with the dog. All I knew was we had just felt something very deep, disturbing in an exciting sort of way.

I couldn't keep my mind on the second act. All I could feel was *danger* in the air. At one point when some Aqua Velva gook of a student was singing "This Nearly Was Mine," I felt like somebody was going to slide into the seat behind me and stab me in the back. Hortense calls me "Paranoid Harry" sometimes and says all writers are psychosomatic. Hortense was sitting next to me making believe she was very interested in *South Pacific*, but I knew her mind—like mine—was still on the mysterious boy. What Hortense does if she's *not* interested in something is sit forward in her seat and look very serious. It fools everybody except me. What was going on in my mind, after I got past the feeling that I was going to be assassinated, was a children's story my mother once read to me when I was four. One of the nicest things about my mom was she used to read to me a lot. It was this story about a king with sixteen gorgeous daughters, and the youngest one was so beautiful she used to freak everyone out. She also used to play with a golden ball, and one day the ball rolled into a lake, but a frog made a deal with the princess that he'd get the ball if she'd take him home with her and let him be her friend and eat with her at the royal dinner table forever and ever. Well, the princess said, "Oh, yes, I promise you anything!" and so the frog dove back into the lake and got the ball for her. But then the princess merely said, "Thank you," took the ball, and started running away like she had never made any deal with the frog at all.

"Come back," the frog called after her. "You said you'd let me be your friend!"

But the princess kept running, so the frog got very angry, jumped out of the lake, and ran after her. He caught her before she got to the palace, dragged her back to the lake, and pulled her underwater to *his* world, which had a lot of exotic fish, crystal tadpoles, and some kind of silver turtle that played a harp. Later I remembered that story and told Hortense. She said my subconscious was warning me about being dragged toward something stronger than myself—an Adventure in the classical sense. Actually, I think that's how great important adventures start for all of us. They come like invitations! Things we chance upon, or perhaps it's something preordained—stronger than chance.

That night, when *South Pacific* was over and the band was packing up their screechy clarinets and tubas, Hortense and I went backstage to congratulate this one girl we knew, Lorraine Newt, who had played one of the natives in the chorus. She was a very sensitive girl who had always been nice to Hortense and me, although we didn't know her very well. So there we were backstage chatting with

18

Lorraine, telling her how much we had enjoyed her per-
formance—while a lot of the other members of the cast
were smoking and illegally drinking beer and screaming
about how fabulously Rocky Funicelli twirled the tassels
on the ends of his coconuts—when I noticed Hortense's
face change suddenly. I turned and saw the boy from the
lobby again. This time he was less than two feet away from
me, and his presence was so powerful, Lorraine Newt simply ran off.

"Hello." The boy smiled. "I'm Jason Rohr."

I looked at Hortense and saw her color deepen. I wanted
to warn her about the frog in my mother's story. No matter
how nice-looking a frog is, it can drag you down deep into
a lake like that frog did to the princess with the golden
ball. But I was really warning myself, too.

> I hear a voice you cannot hear,
>   Which says I must not stay,
> I see a hand you cannot see,
>   Which beckons me away.

That's by Thomas Tickell (1686–1740).

4

When Jason had introduced himself, Hortense did something she doesn't usually do. She smiled right back.

"Hi, I'm Hortense. And this is Harry. We're very glad to meet you," she said.

"Yes," I spoke up. "Harry Hickey and Hortense McCoy."

"I saw you before in the lobby," Jason said, flicking his full mane of light sandy hair out of his eyes.

"We write for the *Bird's Eye Gazette*," I said.

"You *do*?" Jason's eyes looked like they had gone from one hundred kilowatts of energy straight into a million megawatts.

"We're only the theater critics," Hortense humbly explained.

"But once in a while we write short stories and things," I added. "Last month the *Bird's Eye* printed one of my poems—it was called 'Requiem for a Centrifugal Carrot Juicer.' "

"It was a humorous piece," Hortense added.

Jason moved still closer, nearly breathing down our necks.

"*I have a story I need someone to write for me,*" he said, now looking more like he wanted to suck us both up into his two incredibly dark eyeballs!

"What kind of story?" Hortense asked.

"It's a story about a hero," he said.

Hortense and I felt a spark crackle between us. I mean, nothing like out of *The Exorcist* or *Tron* or anything like that. But, it all had to be more than a coincidence! For over a year we'd been saying there were no heroes anymore, and how the world needed heroes and heroines again. I mean, we never really used exactly such archaic terms, but the gist had certainly been there! And then here comes this tall mysterious boy and he wants to tell us a story about a hero! I was just about to ask him what he was doing backstage when the star of the show, June Peckernaw, moved swiftly up and slipped her hand into Jason's.

"Let's get outta here," June twittered, like she was still portraying Nellie Forbush. June Peckernaw is a cheerleader at Hormone High who tries to look like Marilyn Monroe, but she's got a large nose and water-balloon-size knees. She was terribly miscast as Nellie Forbush in *South Pacific*, and she's without a doubt one of the fastest, meanest girls in the junior class. Everyone knows that on Friday nights when a boy drops her off at two A.M., she waves good-bye to him and goes in her front door and straight out the back into *another* boy's van. And one of the dozen guys she's been dating lately has been Rocky Funicelli, who's just as bad as she is.

"I just want to finish my conversation," Jason told June firmly, which shut her right up, so she just stood there with a sour look on her face.

"Could I call you?" Jason asked us.

"Oh, sure," Hortense said too quickly, then took out a pen. He offered her his program to write on, and she scribbled her name and phone number right over the photo of June Peckernaw's face.

"Thanks," Jason said, then wrote his number on our program. *"Please call me,"* he added with a beautiful smile.

"We will," I said emphatically before Hortense could. "Oh, by the way—was that your dog waiting outside the lobby?"

"Yes." Jason beamed at us.

Then June Peckernaw just dragged him off. I heard her say in a stage whisper meant to be overheard, "Why were you talking to *those* clods?" We felt like running after her and yanking her two tons of cascading blond hair, but then we heard Jason defend us.

"Those are great kids," he told her. "I could just see in their eyes that they're smart, *special* . . ."

"He looks like Mikhail Baryshnikov," Hortense whispered to me reverently, "only taller."

Beware the frog, I thought, but didn't say anything.

5

Well, the next day was Saturday, and Hortense called me at eight twenty-three in the morning, which did not thrill me. I was having a dream about being the first fifteen-year-old boy to receive the Tompkinsville Belles Lettres Award for a teenage epic. I dreamed I got it because I wrote a saga set on a tropical island, and all I could remember about it was Einstein, Newton, and Mary Poppins were all shipwrecked together, and they were writing some book about why unhappy wives take so many tennis lessons. But I woke up to Hortense on the phone telling me that Jason Rohr had already called her.

"He wants us to meet him at his house!" she said excitedly.

"O.K.," I said, and we made arrangements to meet at the corner of Milden Avenue and Victory Boulevard, which is where we usually meet unless we're going to school, in which case we meet at Glen Street and Victory. And the reason Hortense's call didn't wake up everyone else in the house was because we each paid for private phones in our own rooms from the very beginning of our friendship. It took a good chunk out of our allowances and a little saving from summer jobs, but Hortense and I had a pact that if one of us needed to talk to the other even in the middle of the night—well, we'd be there.

I got up, washed and dressed, had a glass of chocolate milk and a frozen prefab waffle with artificial maple syrup. When my mother's up she loves to make me breakfast, although I know she feels badly that she can't afford to squeeze fresh orange juice anymore now that they've cut my father's salary in half. Saturday and Sunday mornings they both like to stay in bed late together. I asked my father once just to kid him, "Hey, what do you guys *do* in there so *long?*"

My father didn't give me a silly wink or anything like that. What he said was: "What good is Life if you don't take time to smell the roses?"

By the time I got to Milden Avenue, Hortense was waiting, practically quivering with anticipation.

"Hi," I said.

"Hi," Hortense said, looking very pretty. She was wearing a nice skirt and a red blouse, which meant she had revved up as much pulchritude as she could muster. I was wearing my usual black pants and my T-shirt with the

SUPPORT GUN CONTROL—SHOOT A HUNTER

patch. She immediately grabbed my arm and started leading.

"Jason lives at Four Milden Avenue."

"The end of Milden Avenue?" I gasped.

"Yes."

Now *nobody* really lives exactly down at the end because Milden Avenue ends a few miles from the Arthur Kill at an old linoleum factory, and one year they even kept discontented bulls there. The rest of our town is fairly normal, with low-class houses and regular stunted evergreens like you see in other underprivileged areas. But the end of Milden Avenue was scary. First of all there *were* a few houses near the deserted linoleum factory, but those had the *really* impoverished and demented families in them. There was the famous Brond family, whose kids used to moon the No. 112 bus. And there was one family with a daughter who had a very large head and a great big blackberry patch in her backyard. And once a titanium spaceship was supposed to have landed in that part of town, and it took an Armenian family on board, but you could never find out whether that was true or not.

Anyway, it was spooky walking down that part of Milden Avenue at any hour of the day, especially this early on a Saturday morning. Jason Rohr lived in a house almost at the very end of the street.

"I think we should go back," I told Hortense.

"Why?" she wanted to know, but I could see she was nervous, too.

"Because everyone who lives around here is Looney Tunes, that's why!" I blurted.

"All poor people aren't nuts," Hortense said in her psychiatric-preachy voice.

After a few more blocks, we spotted a rusty mailbox with a 4 nearly hanging off it, and Hortense even started walking right up this overgrown driveway that led to an old junky house quite far off the street.

I stopped right smack in the middle of the driveway when

25

I got a full look at the house. It looked like something out of *The Revenge of the Blood-Licking Ghouls*. It was two stories of sinking, dark-brown wood with a few broken windows covered by Glad Wrap—and the front door was missing!

Jason appeared at the missing front door, with his huge black dog right at his side.

He was wearing a striped sport shirt and jeans. I wish you could have seen the joy on his face.

"Hi! This is Darwin," he said, introducing us to the dog.

"Hi," Hortense said, as the dog ran up to check us out.

"Hi," I said. Darwin gave us a good sniffing session, obviously to protect his master, but Jason snapped his fingers and the giant animal calmed down.

"Come on," Jason said, putting his arms around our shoulders and leading us into the house. "I want you to meet my aunt!"

Just as I had really relaxed about Darwin, I heard what sounded like *three hundred* Hounds of the Baskervilles barking from somewhere close by. I was starting to ask about them when I saw a cackling hag heading for us from the kitchen. Actually all the rooms we could see from the center hall looked exactly the same: messy, cluttered, with irregular pieces of plasterboard and strictly Salvation Army furniture.

"This is my Aunt Maureen." Jason introduced us to the old lady.

"Just call me Mo'," the hag mumbled.

Mo' had a face with nose capillaries like a road map. She must have been almost a hundred years old, and she walked by means of moving one leg and then doing a little pole vault on a cane. She was wearing tattered army pants and a huge blue sweater. As I shook hands with her, I got

26

a whiff of her perfume, which I can best describe as a cross between lilac and atomized bluefish.

"Hi," I said.

"We're going to be working in my room," Jason explained, leading us up a spiral staircase that had been made out of wood slates from old wine crates.

"I'm just finishin' feedin' the dogs," Mo' called, and headed back into the shadows. "Nice meetin' youse."

"Nice meeting you, Aunt Mo'," Hortense and I said, as Darwin moseyed along with Aunt Mo'.

At the very top of the stairs was a large loft with grotesquely inept paintings. They depicted some kind of Indians doing things in front of overgrown temples. In one painting it looked like they were making a fuss over a girl tied to a stone slab, and a piece of yellowing old paper was taped to the bottom of it saying: *Sacrifice of a Virgin*—which is something that would be rather hard to ever have happen at Hormone High.

"My aunt likes to paint ancient Guatemalan ceremonial scenes," Jason said, opening a door and leading us into his digs.

I felt very sad once I got a gander at his room. I felt sad because it looked like eight macrobiotic artists had starved to death there, and maybe a monk or two. His bed was a sheeted mattress on the floor. There was a desk made by laying a big slab of wood over two boxes, and one of those cheap bridge chairs with folding metal legs that looked like a Sanitation Department special. But the room smelled clean, and the prettiest part of the decor was a series of homemade shelves filled with books. You knew whoever lived in this room was a reader, and I was so glad to see *The Fellowship of the Ring*, *Kidnapped*, and a lot of bigger,

27

thicker paperbacks with titles like *Ancient Greek Military Strategies*.

Hortense had strayed nervously to a window, and I heard her gasp, "Oh, my God!"

The sounds of the barking dogs had started up again as I moved to her side, and I saw Mo' below rocking her way toward a dozen long chicken-wire kennels in the far rear of the yard.

"Aunt Mo' likes Great Danes," Jason explained.

The sight of more than twenty horse-size dogs jumping up and down at their fences distinctly gave that impression. Some were black, some brown. Some had their ears clipped like you usually see on a Great Dane, but others had big floppy ears. What was really amazing was that suddenly all the dogs went silent, including Darwin—and you could see it was because Mo' had lifted a finger and was giving them a little lecture.

"Make yourselves comfortable," Jason said, running his hand through his hair. I was afraid he was a bit embarrassed over the house and dogs. Hortense and I didn't want him to feel badly, so we made believe we didn't even notice the decor. She took the Sanitation Department chair, and I sat on the bed like it was just an ordinary Sears, Roebuck top of the line.

"I'm really glad you could come," Jason said. "Take off your shoes. That's what they do in Japan!"

"No, thanks," Hortense and I said simultaneously.

"Be comfortable."

"Oh, we are," Hortense insisted.

I imagined Aunt Mo' downstairs opening all the kennel gates and telling the Great Danes to go eat us.

"Would you like a glass of papaya juice?" Jason offered.

"Sure," I said, thinking that would make him go down

to the kitchen and I could check with Hortense about what we should do.

"That would be pleasant," Hortense agreed.

Jason went right to the windowsill and grabbed a giant bottle of papaya juice, an already-opened quarter pound of butter, and half a loaf of whole wheat bread. He poured us each some juice into clean-enough plastic glasses.

"Don't you refrigerate your juice and butter?" Hortense inquired.

"Oh, no," Jason assured us. "Nature lets you store butter at room temperature. In fact, most bacteria that grow on dairy products are good for you. And papaya juice can last for *weeks*. The ancient Greeks never refrigerated anything."

Hortense looked pale, and I found myself remembering a quote from *Alice in Wonderland*: "Suppose it should be raving mad, after all! I almost wish I'd gone to see the Hatter instead!"

"You said last night that you had a story about a hero?" I shot at him, because this was what we really cared about, or at least I did.

"Oh, yes," Jason said, his eyes lighting up. "I need you to write a story about a hero who is greater than any astronaut, any president, greater than Alexander the Great, or anyone you could possibly think of!"

"Oh?" I said.

"A hero has come at last to save the world," Jason went on, "but he needs you to help tell everybody before it's too late!"

"Who is this hero?" Hortense asked, putting down the glass of papaya juice Jason had thrust into her hand.

"Me," Jason said quietly, even humbly, with a warm smile. *"I* am the one. Do you understand what I'm saying?"

"Oh, yes," we replied. *"We understand, all right. . . ."*

6

Hortense told me later that schizophrenics aren't all like Dr. Jekyll and Mr. Hyde, or the kind who think they're from Mars. She said she figured right off the bat that Jason Rohr fell into the category of the kind of people who believe they're somebody spectacular like Napoleon or Buddha. She once read in a psychology journal that there was an insane asylum in Port Jervis where two old-lady patients both thought they were Mary, the Mother of God. So they had this interesting problem when the two old ladies first met each other in the sanitarium cafeteria. It seems they sat down together and had a nice chat about the weather and oatmeal, until one of the old ladies asked the other one, "What's your name, dearie?"

"Mary, the Mother of God" came the answer.

"But that's *impossible*," the other old lady said. "You see, *I'm* Mary, the Mother of God!"

30

Well, if Hortense remembers correctly, the two old ladies started throwing Jell-O and spaghetti at each other until they were restrained. Then they settled down, and finally one of the old ladies went to one of the nurses and whispered, "Hey, what was the name of Mary, the Mother of God's *mother?*"

And this nurse, who was a nun, told her, "Anne." And then the old lady went running back to the other old lady and said, "Hey, I made a mistake. You ARE Mary, the Mother of God, and I'm *Anne—your mother!*" Then the two old ladies hugged each other and became great friends. But the part Hortense says she likes best was that the old lady who was able to make the change to Anne was the one who got out of the sanitarium first. See, that seems to be the secret for survival whether you're sane or insane— the ability to change—which is also the secret for survival at Hormone High.

Anyway, in Jason's room Hortense *was* nearly about to have an anxiety attack when I finally found my voice again.

"What would you like us to write about you?" I asked Jason, while Hortense had dropped her eyes down to the plastic cup of congealing papaya juice on the floor.

"I know you must think I'm crazy," Jason said.

"Oh no," Hortense said calmly.

"The teachers think I'm crazy at school," Jason said sadly. "They've got all my records from the other schools and places I've been, and I know a lot of the notes are about my unusual mental condition."

Hortense took her pad and pencil out of her purse, crossed her legs, and tried to look as professional as possible. "Just what kind of a story do you want us to write in the *Bird's Eye Gazette?*"

"My story is bigger than the *Gazette!*" Jason stated, now

31

sitting cross-legged like an Indian on the floor.

"It is?" I said quietly.

"Yes."

"How big is it?" Hortense asked.

"It's so big, certain demonic forces may send agents to silence us, just like they killed lots of other people who tried to make America and other countries better."

"Oh." I put my cup of papaya juice on the floor next to Hortense's.

"You see, this is very archetypal and primitive. I think America is involved right now in a situation that is very much like the one the world was in over two thousand years ago when there were deities like Zeus and Artemis on Mount Olympus!"

"In what way?" Hortense asked.

"Well, thousands of years ago nobody believed in anything—just like now. There were problems of freedom and individuality, and a lot of citizens used to wear togas and they'd kill and maim, and sacrifice lambs and bulls so that the gods would forgive them. Animals and slaves were slaughtered by all sorts of monsters that prowled the land."

Jason's voice got louder.

"And young people didn't believe in their country and schools then either, because they knew a lot of the gods were false and the priests of the temples only wanted gold. Corrupt philosophers began to appear everywhere, to exploit their disciples in great baths with courtesans. Today, the deity of selfishness stalks our lands again. All anyone cares about is ME ME ME! No one cares what happens to anyone except himself!"

Now he was shouting! "We're immoral! In chaos! We worship only Narcissus and Bacchus. We're doomed!"

There was a long silence in the room.

"I think we have to be going now," I finally said firmly, standing up.

Jason looked wounded.

"We have a few more minutes," Hortense insisted, signaling me to sit back down. Somehow there did seem to be something vulnerable beneath the volume of Jason's voice, and I knew now Hortense didn't want us to hurt his feelings. He did sound nuts, but I could sense that he liked us, and that we weren't in any true danger. And we really wanted to understand what he thought could help Hormone High, if not the *world*.

"Tell us more," Hortense urged.

Jason relaxed.

"Back in places like ancient Greece there came a time when nobody was working together. Everybody was split apart. Two thousand years ago there was no sense of unity, just like now! Look at our high school! It's worse than the labyrinth needed to hold the Minotaur monster. The hallways are the paths of the maze, and Dean Niboff is just one of the beasts leading the flesh eaters to devour new batches of youths term after term!"

"But what does that have to do with you?" Hortense asked.

"It has to do with my *job*."

"What job?" I asked.

"Well, I'm embarrassed to say this because I can sense you're uncomfortable with me," he said.

"*Please* tell us," Hortense urged, and just then Darwin came running into the room, plopped down, and rested his head on Jason's foot. The dog looked at us with its big mournful eyes.

Jason began to speak more hesitantly, carefully.

"Well, you see, I think it's my purpose to lead everyone

out of the dark labyrinth." He petted Darwin's huge head gently.

"You're here to lead us out?" Hortense repeated.

"Yes, to point the way with threads of light before the monster destroys all. . . ."

"Threads of light?"

"Yes, I'm here to guide you all back to strength again— in our school and our country and ourselves. Isn't that why you came here today?"

He stared at us now, his great dark eyes locked onto ours.

"Isn't that what you felt about me when you first saw me?" he added.

Hortense and I looked at each other, but Jason didn't wait for an answer. He began to shout again: "Harry and Hortense, NOW IS THE TIME! NOT LATER! NOT TOMORROW!"

Both Jason and Darwin were on their feet now, pacing like panthers. Jason's voice grew still more forceful, passionate, and the dog began to whine.

"Our meeting wasn't an accident! Didn't you feel it? Didn't you feel the vibrations coming out of you?" Again he didn't wait for an answer.

"I saw you, knew you were the ones chosen to help me! It's no accident you write for the *Bird's Eye Gazette*! We're going to inspire Hormone High with a new spirit. We're going to lift it up to a new level. Aristotle and Socrates will be proud to teach there! The children of geniuses and kings will *beg* to go there! We can do it!"

He took a long look at us, and even though I knew he was crazy, there was sense in what he wanted.

"Here, look at this," he insisted. "I can explain it all to you with a demonstration!"

34

Jason moved quickly to a broken bureau next to his bed and pulled out a piece of blue chalk. He drew a line across the middle of the bedroom floor, then grabbed a half dozen paperback books and sat down on the floor about five feet from the line—with Darwin right beside him, still occasionally whining.

"See, that blue line is the finish line, and where I am is the starting line. Now each one of these books is going to represent something that means a great deal to you—one of the dreams you have for yourself in Life. Harry, we'll start with you."

I could feel we were beginning to drift under his spell.

"Now Harry, what's one thing you really want to do in Life before you die? What do you want to be?"

"A famous, good writer," I said softly.

"Great! So this first book we'll let represent your writing goal!" he said, setting the book down on the starting line. "Now, you give us one of *your* most important goals, Hortense!"

"I want to be a psychiatrist," Hortense admitted.

"Oh," he said, not sounding particularly thrilled to hear that piece of news, but he took another book. "We'll let this second book represent that goal, and we'll put it at the starting line, too. What's another goal of yours, Harry?"

"I want to be a national chess champion."

"O.K. This third book is that goal. What's another goal from you, Hortense?"

"I want to help people in hospitals."

"Great! This fourth book is that goal. One more, Harry," he asked, getting very excited as he lined up the books in front of him on the starting line.

"I want to be a profound philosopher!"

"And I want to be a global lecturer!" Hortense offered, sort of getting into the game without knowing exactly what was going on.

"Perfect," Jason said. "Now that's enough."

Even Darwin looked happier, pleased with our enthusiasm.

Then Jason spent a minute getting the books all ready.

"O.K., Harry," Jason said, putting his hand on the first book. "This book represents your goal of wanting to be a great writer. *What did you do last week to reach that goal?*"

"I wrote an essay for English class and read a book called *Tobacco Road.*"

"Fine," Jason said. "Then we'll move your book forward a few inches on its way toward the finish line. And what about you, Hortense? This second book represents your goal of wanting to be a psychiatrist. *What did you do last week to reach that goal?*"

"Er," she started, trying to remember. "Er . . . I recorded one of my dreams in a journal I keep—and also started reading a book that explained why Sigmund Freud used to faint every time he passed his father's graveyard."

"Very good," Jason commended her, "and so we'll move *your* book a few inches toward the finish line." Then he turned back to Harry. "Now, Harry, this third book represents your goal of wanting to be a national chess champion. What did you *do* last week to become a chess champion?"

"Nothing . . ." I mumbled.

"O.K.," Jason said, and then he took that book and flung it straight out the window, which started all the Great Danes barking.

"And now you again, Hortense—this fourth book rep-

36

resents your goal to do charity work in hospitals. What did you do last week to help people in hospitals?"

Hortense was stuttering. "Er, er, er . . . nothing. I didn't have time. . . . I thought about doing something, putting in an application somewhere, but . . ."

It was too late. Jason grabbed that book and threw it out the window. "And I don't even have to ask you about the other goals!" Jason suddenly laughed. "Do you get my point?"

"No," I yelled over the din of the barking dogs.

"What I'm telling you is you can sit around all your life dreaming that you're going to be a famous *this* or *that,* but if you don't *do* something about it each day, it doesn't mean anything! You can just take your goals and throw them all out the window! They're not in the race unless you *do* something! You've got to *act!* Do you understand me? *Make things happen!*"

"Oh," I said, understanding.

But just then I heard Aunt Mo' yelling outside at the dogs, and I realized there was something I did want to know. "Where's your mother and father? Do they live here too?" I asked Jason.

For a moment he looked at me like I had asked him the riddle of the Sphinx. Finally, he answered quietly: "There are a lot of things I need to show you and tell you about me before you can write anything that's going to help anybody. We all have to go to the museum tomorrow."

"Look, Jason," I said, "tomorrow is Sunday, and Hortense and I have some very important things to do. . . ."

"Yes." Hortense jumped in. "We just stopped over today to see if we could even consider you for an interview. Our faculty advisor likes more traditional pieces for the *Bird's*

Eye Gazette, actually, and we're very busy. We've got to get going, but thank you for the papaya juice. . . ."

"Oh, I'm sorry," Jason said, suddenly terribly sad. He tried to smile as though he wasn't hurt. But his shining eyes faded entirely as we got up to leave. He knew that we had no intention of writing any history about him, and that we both thought he was bonkers.

"Do you think you might be able to go to the museum with me *someday?*" Jason asked, in a tone I could only describe as begging.

"We've got deadlines," I said, taking Hortense's arm and walking her out toward the rickety spiral staircase.

In the hallway Jason rushed past us to the stairs, and Darwin almost knocked us over.

"Let me go first," he said. "If you trip, I'll catch you."

"Thank you," Hortense said, smiling at him.

"I've been going to the museum a lot lately." Jason sighed as we all went down the stairs.

"You like . . . the paintings?" Hortense inquired.

"I go to see all the ancient Greek exhibits. The antique spears and statues. And I spend a great deal of time with my *father.* . . ."

"Your father?" I asked.

"Yes. My *real* father."

"Where is he?" Hortense asked.

"In the museum."

"Is he the caretaker?" I inquired.

"Oh, no," Jason laughed.

In a moment we were all outside on the dilapidated porch, but I couldn't leave without knowing exactly what his father did at the museum. I asked Jason directly.

"I'm afraid to tell you," he confessed.

"You can tell us," Hortense said softly to him.

"They have a whole room full of my father's things at the museum," Jason explained. "My father was very famous, but he's dead now."

"What was your father's name?" Hortense asked carefully.

Jason smiled proudly. "You'll find out," he said. And there was something about the way he said those words that was both tantalizing and chilling.

"O.K.," Hortense said, and then we were both practically running down the driveway to flee far, far away from Milden Avenue and this strange, sad, crazy kid.

7

Right after we left Jason's house, we went to the Century Shopping Plaza, where they make these giant Grandma Dork's Chocolate Chip Cookies and you can hang out at a bench and drink a cup of coffee.

"Jason Rohr *is* crazy," Hortense whispered as we nibbled on our eight-inch-diameter cookies and a lot of kids from Hormone High strolled by with shopping bags filled with what we knew would be mainly five-finger-discount stuff.

"He's crazy," I said. "But he's not dull."

"We're not really going to help him write any story," Hortense said. "How could we!"

I let Hortense talk on because she always does that when something makes her nervous, and I knew that the thought of Jason Rohr was disturbing her. I knew he was a nut, but there was something extra original about him. Then when

40

she said, "But he *is* a fascinating case study," I knew very well where we'd both be going the next day. Within an hour we had called Jason to tell him we *would* meet him at the museum.

What a Sunday.

Hortense and I arrived about ten minutes early at the Staten Island Brighton Museum and sat on a bench outside right next to a statue of a man with no head that looked like it had been made by Son of Sam. And right next to that one was a massive bronze old man in a cloak, but his hands were broken off. This plaque said what happened was that the sculptor, Rodin, showed the original statue *with hands* to some of his students, and they all said the hands were too big, so Rodin just chopped them off, and now the statue is worth much more because it has that interesting dramatic story connected to it.

Hortense spent the whole time we waited combing her China doll hair straight down and checking her face in a reflection from a chrome sundial. She even put on a very, very red lipstick.

"Making up for the lunatic?" I asked.

"Are you jealous?"

"Nope."

"He's handsome."

"Yes," I told her. "You can just drop me, go marry him, and some night you'll wake up calling me to help you out of some Greek labyrinth."

I *was* annoyed at her for making herself look extra beautiful today! She wore this weird-style dress that looked like a toga, like she was getting into the spirit of Grecian history—or into the spirit of Jason's history, anyway. I was

41

wearing a cap that said MOZART on the front, because I didn't want Jason to think I was ignorant of fine art.

Jason arrived at ten minutes after eleven, dressed in shorts and a blood-red T-shirt.

"Hi," he said with his strange, sad smile.

"Hi," I said.

"Did you bring your notebooks?" he wanted to know.

Hortense produced a small black box from her handbag.

"I brought my tape recorder."

"Great!" Jason said.

He led us up the front steps two at a time, and gave the revolving entrance door such a shove I had to skip so I wouldn't be crushed. Then we paid fifty cents each to an old lady who looked like Whistler's Mother at a turnstile. She thanked us and told us each paid admission entitled us to a map of the three floors of the museum and a free postcard-size copy of an oil painting that looked like it should have been called *German Husbands Doing Housework*.

"What are we going to see first?" Hortense wanted to know.

"Well, we start with my favorite paintings and sculptures from the modern period, then the Egyptian room—and after that we'll be ready for what I *really* want to show you."

"O.K.," we said.

I must say Jason knew the museum. The very first painting he took us to gave me the creeps. It was called *Spring*, and it was by Giuseppe Arcimboldo, who died in 1593. It was a lady's profile, and every part of her was made of flowers. The artist gave her a shoulder made of a cabbage, an ear made of a rose, and a face that looked like a prickly pear. I really wanted to upchuck, but that was nothing compared to what was coming. The next painting Jason

42

showed us was called *The Three Graces*—a trio of girls who looked like they had spent too many afternoons at The Leaning Tower of Pizza. But the next painting was really freaky. This one had a French title I couldn't understand: *Le temps ou les vieilles*—but Jason said it was something like Time or the Old Women by Francisco de Goya. It was mainly a portrait of what looked like two undernourished, underdressed bag ladies.

"What do you think about when you see these paintings?" Hortense asked, holding her tape recorder up to record Jason's response.

"A lot of things," he said, sounding very pensive.

"They make *me* think of Death," I blurted out, and Hortense shot me a dirty look.

After about a half hour of more bizarre paintings, Jason walked us swiftly through some of the weirder galleries. The only original item our museum has that makes it somewhat unique is the largest sea-gull cyclorama in the world. It's in a very long room, and the back wall is curved with a pretty sky and ocean painted on it, and they have stuffed dusty sea gulls in various positions. There's a button you press, and a recorded voice tells you: *There are more than twenty-eight different species of gulls that make Staten Island their home. Sea gulls have been seen picking clams out of the local tide pools and flying high into the air to drop them onto rocks in order to crack them: This allows our sea gulls to eat. . . .*

After that, Jason and Hortense were starting into the Egyptian Room, but I spotted a special exhibit on FASCINATING FACTS AND UNEXPLAINED PHENOMENA. I let them go ahead because some of the facts were so incredible I had to jot them down. I knew it would be my duty as a writer to integrate them into literature one day so the whole world

43

could know what unusual and wonderful things can happen in life. Here's a list of ten of them; and they're all absolutely true and reported in famous newspapers:

1) On the 23rd of September in 1973 ten thousand small toads fell from the sky in a "freak storm" onto the southern French village of Brignoles.

2) In 1911 a picture of Christ in a church at Mirebeau, France, began bleeding, and tests done at London's Lister Institute showed the blood to be a very rare human type. Also, in Sicily a picture of the Madonna started to weep. (The Brighton Museum has about four other examples of mysterious flows and oozings.)

3) Mr. and Mrs. Swain drive 100 miles each weekend to find a lake they once saw but it disappeared. They said the lake had a big boulder in the middle of it that had a sword sticking out of it.

4) A fisherman off Nantucket Island in 1962 lost his set of Volvo keys in the ocean. Six weeks later a codfish swam up to his boat and spat them out to him.

5) In one year, hens in America lay enough eggs to encircle the earth a hundred times.

6) Castor oil is used as a lubricant in jet planes.

7) Midgets almost always have normal-sized children.

8) Every year more people are killed in Africa by crocodiles than by lions.

9) A hippopotamus can run faster than a man.

10) President Taft weighed 352 pounds.

Now, that's the kind of museum data that really interests me. I got so caught up in that display, I came in at the tail end of Jason and Hortense's stroll through the Egyptian exhibit. I had been to the Egyptian room once before, when Mrs. Haines took my eighth-grade class on a school outing, and I remembered most of it. The museum doesn't make too many changes over the years, and they only have one *Homo sapiens* mummy. Jason and Hortense were sitting right in front of it when I found them. It was eerie because the mummy is a boy, and he's partially unwrapped and not the kind of thing you want to see. Jason was talking now, but not to Hortense or me. He was talking right into the tape recorder, and an old guard was standing nearby watching.

"This boy was a prince of Egypt when he died, and hundreds of servants were sacrificed and buried with him so that in the afterlife he would have company. Being alone is the worst thing that can happen to a human being," Jason said. "And just imagine how lonely it is to be a *god*. . . ."

Then he caught sight of me, as though for a moment he had forgotten I even existed.

"The Greek exhibit is on the top floor," he said, leading the way up a staircase. Hortense and I could barely keep up with him.

"He *is* crackers, you know," I just had to remind her.

"Oh, shut up," she said, shoving her hand over my mouth.

There wasn't a soul on the third floor except some guard who looked like he had just switched from being a janitor in a crematorium. You could tell he hated kids and probably got his mean-looking mouth from saying, "Hey, don't touch that," to forty million pupils whose teachers had made them come to the museum under threat of scholarly death.

Anyway, the third floor of the Staten Island Brighton Museum was the spookiest part of the joint because it's sort of dark and these shafts of light come shooting across the huge rooms from small dungeonlike windows set high

45

in the walls. "Just let the silence surround you," Jason advised. It *was* very still.

Hortense reached out for my hand.

The first exhibit we stopped to look at was a painting called *The Time of the Warrior-Kings*—which showed a million people stabbing each other and locking folks in golden torture chambers.

"Thousands and thousands of years ago Greece knew more than we do now," Jason said, moving us on to a glass display case that held a gold mask of a Greek fighter who had lived more than 3500 years before and had boiled half a town in oil. Then they had these pieces of pottery and parts of old walls that showed things like King Agamemnon standing ready for battle, and Ajax, a leading Greek wrestler, retrieving the body of his slain comrade Achilles; and there were other cases with some really bizarre jewelry the Greek ladies used to wear. One was a bee pendant; another was an octopus-shaped necklace— and the third was a pair of waterbug earrings. Then came an exhibit that made Hortense especially nervous. I could tell, because she nearly tripped and dropped her tape recorder. This section was called MYTHIC MONSTER KILLERS! It showed a lot of things like a naked guy on a horse that had a goat's head growing out of its back. Then there was a big piece from a temple showing a young man called Perseus slitting the throat of Medusa, who was a monster who had snakes for hair. And there were a lot of typewritten explanations under the statues and things, which told all about things like "the creation myth," and "the birth of Zeus" and why people long ago had to believe in all those crazy gods and monsters. They even had more horrible creatures in those days than we have at Hormone High; but we have no gods or heroes to protect us.

Suddenly Jason halted.

"There are no brave people anymore," Jason said simply, reverently.

"Some firemen and policemen are brave," Hortense said matter-of-factly.

"Not the kind who would face the great monsters of our world."

"What about some of the teachers at our school who face the kids?" I offered.

Jason was not amused.

"Well, Mr. Olsen tries," said Hortense, who is always fair.

Jason led us into a huge, shadowy, dome-shaped room that had other paintings depicting the exploits of ancient Greek heroes. There was one of Hercules knocking off a bunch of centaurs—which as you know are half man, half horse. And there was another, smaller painting of some god who looked a bit like Neptune whacking the tail off Charlie the Tuna. Then suddenly Jason took hold of us and made us sit on a stone bench under the middle of the spooky dome. There in front of us now was a huge painting that reached far up the wall and was at least twenty feet across. It had a man with feathers glued to his arms, and he was flying. Just above him was a boy who also had wings, but his were beginning to fall apart.

"Look closely at the older man," Jason ordered, still holding our arms very tightly. "Look at his face, his powerful wings!"

"We see him," I said, trying to work my arm out of his grasp. Hortense didn't even *try* to struggle loose. She just stared up at the painting, and I could tell she didn't dare move even a strand of hair.

"*That is my father,*" Jason said, and his eyes glistened. "My father, *Daedalus*. . . ."

"Oh," Hortense and I said.

"And see the young boy above, the one flying too close to the sun and beginning to fall? That's *me! Me! Icarus!*"

Then Jason Rohr simply, uncontrollably burst into tears.

Hortense and I just looked at each other. Hortense gave him a hug I'm sure she meant to be comforting, and I stood up to block him from the view of a couple of tourists who came walking by at one point. Then Jason got hold of himself, said, "Excuse me," and disappeared into the men's room.

Hortense stood up next to me.

"Jason is *very* ill," she said.

"I think you're jumping to conclusions," I said.

Hortense was too upset to catch the sarcasm.

"A boy tells us his father is *Daedalus*, and you think I'm jumping to conclusions!"

"I thought you had compassion for the mentally disturbed," I reminded her. "And besides, maybe he's only testing us."

"*Testing* us? He's out of his mind." Hortense sounded frightened. "He thinks his father is a man out of a multi-thousand-year-old myth? Daedalus *never even lived!*"

I must say I had never seen Hortense so freaked out before, but in a moment Jason was back, and the three of us just sat in silence on the bench, with Hortense staring at the floor. Finally she said, "Why did you post those notes from 'Icarus, a god' at school?"

"It's too late," he said miserably.

I could see Hortense softening as she gazed into his still-tear-filled eyes.

"Too late for what?" I asked.

"Too late to escape from the labyrinth," he said.

"But the things you've done, the things you're thinking, are not *normal*," Hortense leveled with him, in a voice filled with pity. I thought she should have kept her mouth shut for a while.

"If only you'd just listen to me," Jason pleaded. "Listen to more of what I've got to say."

"Of course we'll listen to you," I spoke up.

"Maybe if I could just say what I need everyone to know into your tape recorder," Jason nearly begged again now. "Maybe you could just type it out for me. There's too many thoughts in my head and I can't write them all down— that's why I need you." Jason was really focused on Hortense now and I could see her really *wanting* to help.

"But you're disturbed. You need counseling," she told him sincerely. "You *aren't* Icarus, Jason! You aren't a god!"

"They always think smart people are disturbed. Don't you think our high school and world need a leader who is wise and good?" Jason asked.

"Sure, but . . ."

"Then listen to me. That's all I'm asking," he said, reaching out to take the tape recorder. "I never pretended to be the supreme God of the Universe," he added.

"You're just 'Icarus, a *little* god'?" I inquired.

"A demigod," Jason explained humbly. "That's a god who is half man, who can help people find the god in themselves."

Hortense was beginning to look faint, so I suggested we all go get a little fresh air.

We went downstairs to the first floor, and back outside, and sat near the statue of the bronze guy with no hands. I could see Hortense really wanted to clear out, but I zapped her with my eyes, which always works. She just accepted matters, and Jason started talking into the tape recorder around two-thirty and completely filled up sixty minutes of tape. We just sat there listening to him until the tape ran out. And even after that we sat quite a while longer, dazed, as Jason pleaded with Hortense to take the tape home and type up what he'd said, because he really needed it. A lot of it Hortense and I didn't even understand, because our minds were flying around from the bizarreness of the whole thing, and we could still see the huge painting of Daedalus emblazoned in our minds. He talked a lot about how our country no longer cherishes its children, how family life is dead, and how most parents are just sitting around watching T.V. and waiting to be vaporized in a thermonuclear blast. "Kids are a blessing!" I remember he said, and there were tears in his voice. He seemed to be pleading with us. Of course, I saw the step-by-step change in Hortense's scientific attitude as Jason directed most of his story to her. I've always been jealous of boys like Jason who had black eyes and black eyebrows and blond hair. I knew if I looked like that I'd be an actor and not a writer or a theater critic. And Jason would reach out and touch Hortense and me at all the right times. He could grab a hand or give a hug to connect with us. There, outside the museum, on a plain cold cement bench, he was dealing with Hortense like he was a great hero and she was a goddess. She was responding, too—and it reminded me of a poem about a goddess who descends into a dark and dangerous world.

> My lady abandoned heaven, abandoned earth,
>   To the nether world she descended . . .

"I suppose I *could* transcribe the tape," Hortense finally said, now completely hypnotized by Jason.

"*Would* you? *Would* you do that for me?" Jason lit up.

"Sure she would," I said angrily.

"What time could I pick up the pages?" Jason wanted to know—but it wasn't until Monday morning that we found out what he was going to do with them! He put them straight up on the main Hormone High bulletin board! And at the end after his signature, "Icarus, a god," he wrote: "I have two new friends who will help me bring my truth to you—Harold Hickey and Hortense McCoy!"

8

Hortense was horrified to find out Jason had used the pages she typed for him as his next bulletin message from "Icarus, a god." We tried to find Jason, but Dean Niboff's secretary, Miss Brogan, found us first. She interrupted our biology teacher's demonstration of electrotropism in a paramecium to tell us Dean Niboff wanted to see us both immediately.

"What for?" I wanted to know as Miss Brogan led us down to Room 110.

"I can't say," Miss Brogan replied softly. But we guessed, of course.

Miss Brogan was one of the sweetest secretaries in the school, and she always looked mature and gracious. She wore dark linen suits with an oyster-shell cameo pin, which she told Hortense she had bought on a 1963 float into the Blue Grotto at Capri, Italy.

Dean Niboff was on the phone when she led us through

her small outer workroom into his larger, heavily paneled office.

"Please have a seat," she said, indicating these two squatty Leatherette chairs in front of the Dean's desk. We did as we were told, and felt like we were being locked in a crypt as she smiled and went out to her typing desk, sealing the door behind her.

We sat there waiting; then I could see Hortense had decided to perk up into a body language that would show Dean Niboff she had done nothing wrong. Of course, Dean Niboff's face alone was a fearsome thing. He was a short man, about fifty-five, with a booming voice, and looked just like one of those judges from a movie who condemns someone to die in a gas chamber. He also had jowls the size of Winston Churchill's, which wiggled when he jerked his head—which he did a lot of, particularly during the last stages of his phone conversation, which sounded from his end as if he had just given the okay for seventy-three teenage lobotomies.

Finally he hung up, sat back in his huge swivel chair, and looked at us with his owlish bloodshot eyes.

"How do you know Jason Rohr?" he demanded to know.

"He introduced himself to us, sir," Hortense said respectfully.

"Why are your names on this?" he wanted to know, waving the latest "Icarus, a god" notice at us, with "Icarus, a god" giving us credit at the end.

"I don't know, sir," I lied.

"Oh, I *typed* it, Dean Niboff," Hortense said, "but I didn't know he was going to put our names on it and tack it up!"

"You know how he signs these?" Dean Niboff stressed.

"Yes, sir."

"Is that one of your aspirations in life, Miss McCoy—to be a 'god's' typist?"

"No, sir. Jason just seems to be a very nice, intelligent boy who needs friends very badly."

"So did Jack the Ripper," Dean Niboff grunted. "*Are* you his friends?"

"Not really. We hardly know him," I said quickly.

"But we feel someone should help him."

"Then I have some advice for you," Dean Niboff offered, with a shake of his jowls.

"What, sir?"

"Don't touch him with a ten-foot pole."

"Why not?"

"Because *I said you shouldn't.* Jason Rohr is a very disturbed young man and I agreed to take him into this school strictly on a probational status. He's been kicked out of dozens of others. I have warned him that one more stunt like this and he's out of here, too. We have enough problems without having 'Icarus, a god' on campus. And did you know he brings a giant black mutt with him every day that sits out front waiting for him?"

"Yes, sir," Hortense admitted. "And he's not a mutt. He's a Great Dane. His name is Darwin."

"Exactly what's wrong with Jason, sir?" I pursued.

"None of your business. I checked your records. You're both fine students who do not need a banana for a friend."

"But we think he needs *us,*" Hortense said. "He seems so lonely."

"Do you understand English?"

"Yes, sir."

"Then go back to class. I doubt if Jason Rohr will last another week at our school, and I assume you don't need me to call your parents about this matter?"

54

"No, sir," Hortense mumbled.

"Have you told them you've been associating with a lunatic?"

"No, sir," I said.

"Then it's settled."

"Yes, sir," we both sputtered.

I zipped out my chair first and dragged Hortense up, and in a flash we were scooting by Miss Brogan's rapidly typing fingers. Just then the bell rang, ending the sixth period, and in another moment we were lost in a horde of Hormone High kids pushing and shoving through the hall.

That afternoon we were the last ones to hang around the *Bird's Eye Gazette* office. Mr. Olsen had left us to close up shop. He said he had to catch a three forty-five ferry boat to Manhattan because an old copy-editor friend he knew had invited him to have dinner at the Pen Club, which he told us is the kind of establishment where a lot of newspaper people go and do fabulous things like trade witty bon mots and journalistic memories over double brandies and other exotic drinks. So it was just Hortense and me in the office feeling very depressed because we really didn't like being told we *had* to stay away from Jason, and we were even more afraid of what Dean Niboff would do to him. I mean, it wasn't that we didn't know Jason had a few mental quirks, but he really needed us to care about him. Imagine living with Aunt Mo'! Where *were* his own real parents? And why did he have to invent Daedalus for his father? All he had was that crazy dog and his bulletins the kids laughed at so much! He seemed mainly super-lonely. I mean, that's why most kids to unusual, weirdo things. Kids shave their heads and dye their ears purple and wear peacock-feather earrings and all those things a lot of times just so they'll be noticed. Hortense and I were lucky be-

55

cause we had found a "socially acceptable" way of getting attention with our reviews and my maniacal essays in the *Bird's Eye Gazette*! And we had our parents behind us! Also, we were furious about the way Dean Niboff had checked us out in the records. He really had acted like he was a J. Edgar Hoover or head of the KGB and we were double agents.

"That Niboff had some nerve checking our records," I said, doing imitations of jowl shaking. Hortense half smiled.

Then she turned serious. "You've got your devilish elf look," she said, "What are you thinking?"

"Nothing," I said, grabbing her hand and pulling her out into the now-deserted hall. Only a couple of kids were on the whole third floor by this time, and that was because the after-school chess club was meeting in Room 309 and they only have two members at Hormone High. I dragged Hortense down two flights of stairs before she dared guess what I was up to.

9

The records room is on the first floor connected to the main office, and when we got there all the office doors were wide open with two of the assistant custodians throwing disinfectant-soaked sawdust around so they'd have something to sweep up. One assistant was called Danny, and he was pushing this huge three-foot-wide broom up and down the inner office near the switchboard. Danny looks a little like a retarded version of John Travolta, with these large ears and a constant smile that creates the effect that he's just had an electroshock treatment. His buddy, the other assistant custodian, is Ricky, who's short and stocky and looks like he's in a constant dream state thinking about where his next baked lasagna is coming from. Anyway, we told them we had to distribute some notices in the teachers' mailboxes and file our program cards, all of which we knew would tax their mental powers, so we just made believe we were checking passes and things. We found a stack of twofer theater tickets on the main counter and kept busy shuffling those until both assistant custodians had plenty of sawdust to sweep up, and then we slid into the open records room. I ran for the R file and yanked at the drawer, but it was locked. Hortense looked on the verge of cardiac arrest as I mimed for her to wait while I dashed out right by Ricky, telling him I heard the Chunk-E-Cheese pizza parlor was giving a free eight-inch pizza with every eleven-inch ordered with two or more extra ingredients. I slipped the records cabinet keys from the top left-hand drawer of Mrs. Reilland's desk, where I knew she always kept them. In there also was a stash apple some kid had forgotten to pick up. I know where they keep the computer codes for the fire drills and atomic attack routines, but right now all I really needed was the keys. I'd never taken anything like this before, except once I borrowed a ream of typing paper from the supply room because I had been planning to write my first novel, which I was going to call *Justice, My Donkey*—but I never did. I felt there was something about Jason Rohr we had to know if we were going to have any chance to help him. And I knew Hortense would never just stand by and let Dean Niboff railroad *anybody* unless they really deserved it. Jason may have been nuts, but he was a good, well-intentioned kind of nut.

I deliberately rattled the keys as I went back by Ricky and Danny this time. They knew I always had Mr. Olsen's keys from the *Bird's Eye Gazette*, and I strolled into the records room like I had been sent there on some very sophisticated official business.

Hortense was green leaning against a file, straining to see out the windows.

"What if a grade advisor is working late?" she whis-

58

pered, as I unlocked the R cabinet and rolled it open like a slab at the morgue.

"No sweat."

I ran my fingers rapidly over the R's, but Hortense knew alphabetizing had never been one of my strong points. She pushed me to the side and had pulled out Jason's file in a second. We'd seen a lot of other kids' files over the years when we worked for service credits from grade advisors, but this one was really crammed with notations and extra documents. There were a lot of red failure grades in the marking sections with all the little yellow checking squares, and I saw a mass of scribbling in the other areas. Also, there were a few long typed letters written on institution-type stationery, and a note from at least one shrink. But then finally, on the third page of the large main record itself, was the handwritten red-ink information we had been looking for. In clear legible script it told us that when Jason Rohr was six years old, his father had *murdered his mother* and then killed himself. "The boy was then sent to live with his father's older sister," the form said.

Hortense and I stared at each other. *Aunt Mo'!*

Well, the moment we read *that*, we split from the record room and that school so fast, the assistant custodians must have thought we'd just seen a corpse. Of course, in a sense we had—a *double* corpse—and we ran all the way to Century Shopping Plaza.

When we reached the mall it wasn't crowded, so we bought two coffees and a couple of the giant cookies, and sat on one of the benches. We hadn't said a word yet. Hortense just stared into space while I chugalugged my coffee. I went to the counter and bought us a couple of Grandma Dork's Raspberry Chip Brownies. I stuck one of the brownies in her hand and watched her nibbling on it.

"I don't know how to explain it," I said softly, not wanting to upset her even further, "but I still think we're both being called to a very special Adventure. There's something we're being called on to do. Something not just for Jason—but because of him—of what he wants to stand for! Are you interested in tracking Jason down at his house?"

"No."

"Hortense, he *needs* us! It's not like you."

"Dean Niboff told us to keep away from him! My God, his father *murdered* his mother! And then committed suicide!"

I raised my voice so she'd think I knew what I was talking about. "If we don't go find him we'll be refusing our Call."

"What Call? The Call of the Traumatized Nut?"

"If you didn't read so many psych books, you'd be more open to *magic!*"

"Jason Rohr is not magic. He's a desperate mental case!"

"Don't you know what happens to kids who don't answer the Call when it comes into their lives?" I challenged her.

"Yes. They live longer."

"No. They turn into people like Dean Niboff."

"*You're* crazy."

"No."

"Yes."

"Hortense, I've been meaning to tell you this lately, but we've become as bad as all the others. We're the ones trapped in a maze. We haven't done anything courageous, not like this, ever. We haven't tried to change the things we hate. We've been writing and criticizing too much and not living enough. You can't become a great writer or shrink without getting out, caring about other people, and taking chances for them!"

60

"Jason Rohr's way over our heads, Harry!"

"You're the one who was gaga over him."

"I was not gaga!"

I let her alternate nibbles on her chocolate chip cookie and brownie, while some denizens from Hormone High started parading by with their shopping packages and fried brains. One girl from my biology class called Tammy Motts and another girl by the name of Cloris Zapp sat down at a table near us and started talking about learning how to use iridescent eyeliner and the latest plot development on *The Young and the Restless.*

"I want to go home," Hortense said.

"But we have to talk about Jason."

"No, we don't!"

And this time she really meant it.

I didn't get home that night until around five-thirty, and my mother was preparing a meat loaf. When my mother prepares meat loaf she looks a little like a woman trying to beat the life out of an abalone, and she throws a lot of parsley, onion, and Hamburger Helper into the thing so that by the time it hits the dinner table it looks like a souvenir from the petrified forest. She tells us each recipe is a specialty from a famous person, so that if it tastes awful we can blame *them.* She makes things like Eleanor Roosevelt dumplings, Bob Hope stuffed flounder, and The Fonz pork chops. Actually, I have to admire the way Mom has adjusted to being *nouveau poor.*

"How was school today?" she asked me.

"A fabulous experience."

"What did you do after school?" she pursued.

"Hung around the mall."

"I hope you were careful. I read that someone shot somebody in a mall last week in Cleveland."

"We didn't go to Cleveland."

"Don't be rude."

"I'm not being rude. I mean, all the kids go there and have a Salad-in-a-Pita."

"Somebody shot eight people in a diner last week," Mom added, as she gave the meat loaf a few last slaps. "Two men came in with stocking caps and, for no reason at all, started shooting at all the people at the counter."

By six-thirty my father had come home and we were sitting around the dinner table. He was very depressed, which he's been a lot lately ever since he was put in charge of the "Sugar Is Good for You" advertising account at his agency.

His firm used to handle a sugar-substitute account, so he used to have to write ad copy that said "Sugar Is Bad for You." He dug up all these statistics at that time that showed that we all eat about ninety-seven pounds of sugar a year and how sugar rots our teeth and gives us all kinds of disease. He did such a good job writing ads *against* sugar that the sugar companies now paid the agency twice as much to drop the sugar-substitute account and take on sugar instead. That's what's really depressed him. For the last two months he's had to help invent a lot of lies so that people won't know they eat ninety-seven pounds of sugar each year and if they *do* know it, convince them it's *good* for them. Five years ago the agency put my pop in charge of a salt account where they had him dig up all the facts about why the over seventy pounds of salt each person eats per year is really healthy for them. In other words, my pop has to lie for whatever company gives him an account, and that's why I think he takes so long to come home from work a lot of nights. But in spite of all my folks' shortcomings, all through dinner all I could think of was how lucky

I was to *have* parents, and how sorry I felt for Jason Rohr. And most of all, no matter how it came out, I had to admit—and still do—that my Mom and Dad always loved me. They're just a little sad.

After the ten-o'clock news the phone rang and I knew it would be Hortense. We have almost an ESP connection, especially when there's something important buzzing between us.

"Hello?" I said.

"Harry?" I heard Hortense's low, guilty voice. "I was thinking," she said, "maybe we *could* go see Jason after school tomorrow. Really try to interview him . . . uh . . . in depth."

"Well, I think we've got nothing to lose."

"Except our lives."

"Do you really think he's dangerous?" I asked.

"It's a possibility." Hortense sighed. "I've read about people like him."

"Then why do you want to go?"

"I don't know," Hortense admitted. "I just don't know. He needs help, I guess."

"Shall I call him?" I inquired.

"I already did," Hortense said, "but he wasn't home. Aunt Mo' said he and Darwin had gone out for a walk to look at the moon and stars. She said sometimes they stay out all night just looking up at the sky!"

10

Jason didn't call Hortense back that night, and the next day we didn't see him anywhere at school. By the time we got out and back to town on the bus, it was late afternoon with the setting sun causing a lot of sharp shadows to fall across Milden Avenue as we headed for his house. I kept expecting something horrible like an ax murderer or the girl with the big head to come running out at us. At this hour of the day Aunt Mo's house looked a bit like something out of the Chain Saw Massacre, and when Aunt Mo' herself appeared in the driveway, she would have given the Bride of Frankenstein a run for her money.

"How was school today?" Aunt Mo' wanted to know. "My Jason played the hook!"

We could barely hear her above the barking dogs, and suddenly giant Darwin came tearing around the corner of the house and jumped up on Hortense, licking her face.

"*Down, Darwin!*" Jason ordered, as he appeared on the front porch, laughing. "He won't hurt you, Hortense! Really."

Darwin finished with Hortense and started licking me, but I gave out a phony growl, which Darwin seemed to really enjoy. Finally he jumped up on Jason, licking his face, too.

"What a nice dog," I said.

"A real pal!" Jason agreed. "The best!"

Aunt Mo' started yelling for Darwin to "get in the back for ya food, critter," and chased him back to the kennels while Jason led Hortense and me toward his room again.

"When I came home last month, Darwin licked my face for three hours," Jason said.

"Home from where?" Hortense wanted to know.

"I'll tell you about that later," Jason said. "I'm so glad you changed your minds about interviewing me," he added.

We went up the spiral staircase and past the room stacked with Mo's weird Guatemalan sacrifice paintings. In Jason's room I saw some other bottles on the windowsill, along with what looked like the same loaf of bread and glob of butter.

"Want some pear nectar?" Jason asked this time.

"No thanks," Hortense and I said in unison.

"At least take your shoes off and make yourselves comfortable."

"O.K."

"O.K."

Jason watched me echo Hortense, and I could see he sensed we were still uncomfortable. He looked afraid we might leave at any moment.

"See, I *had* to take you down to the museum so you'd feel the vibrations of what I'm about, and understand why I need your help so much," Jason started quickly.

"Why do you need our help?" I asked.

"First I need to know if you think I'm insane," Jason asked in a low voice. "In the last school I went to, they thought I was crazy, took me away from Aunt Mo', and put me in a nuthouse."

"Why?" asked Hortense.

"Because I knew I was somebody important and they didn't believe me. By the way, you'd better start taping this," he added.

Hortense took her tape recorder out of her school pack and officially started the interview.

"Did you tell them your father was Daedalus and he put feathers on his arms and tried to fly a few thousand years ago?" Hortense inquired.

"No, I wasn't nuts enough to tell them that," Jason said, smiling.

"Then how did they know you were crazy?" I asked.

"I'm *not* crazy," Jason blurted, and I realized I hadn't really been very smart to ask the question that way.

"Do you mind if we ask who your mother was?" Hortense went on.

"She was someone very special—a goddess," Jason said with great reverence.

"Your mother was a goddess? And she was married to Daedalus?" Hortense pursued.

"No. My mother was a modern goddess, and she was married to another man and they used to live in Edison, New Jersey. But this man she was married to was an evil man, and she told me from as long as I was with her that he wasn't my real father, although he always said he was. She told me Daedalus was my real father and that he was a god. I know it sounds crazy, but she was telling me the truth. Did you see the face on Daedalus' son in the painting?

66

I look just like the son of Daedalus, the one who flew too close to the sun and fell into the ocean. Daedalus' son's name was Icarus. And that's what I think my real name is, actually," said Jason.

Hortense and I exchanged a glance that told me we were both remembering what had *really* happened to Jason's mother and father.

"If you're over two thousand years old, why aren't you dead?" Hortense asked softly.

"My mother said I was reincarnated," Jason explained. "She believed in reincarnation. She said she had made a mistake marrying this man in Edison, New Jersey. But the good part was that she was fertilized by Daedalus. Daedalus was my father."

"That would require a three-thousand-year-old mythological sperm bank," I said.

"No, I told you my mother was a goddess," he said, growing agitated.

"*Was?*" Hortense picked up.

"Yes. She died when I was six," Jason admitted, and here we thought Jason might be getting ready to tell us the full, chilling truth.

"How?" I asked.

"In . . . a car . . . accident," he stuttered.

I could see Hortense wanted to kick me for putting him on the spot with my last question. What it did was make Jason shut up like a clam about his mother and this "evil guy" from Edison, New Jersey. Jason just went silent and sat on the bed, putting his head in his hands. I felt terrible.

After a moment Hortense moved to sit next to him, and put her arm around him. I wasn't even jealous, he looked so sad.

"Maybe I *will* have a glass of pear nectar," Hortense

said, and a smile shot across Jason's face.

In a flash he was at the windowsill pouring away and happily smearing some of the putrid butter on a piece of stale bread.

"Was it an 'evil force' that put you in the institution?" Hortense asked quite seriously, but you could see she was using one of her psychology techniques.

"Yes!" Jason blurted, handing Hortense her nectar and snack.

"Now," Hortense went on to Jason, "on Sunday you were telling us that everybody's just interested in themselves—that nobody really cares what's happening to the world . . . and our schools. How nobody cherishes children anymore . . ."

"Yes! And last night I had a vision!"

"What vision?"

"The clear vision that I need you to help write more letters for me," Jason said soberly. "I think I can give everyone a purpose again, a belief that Life is good and has meaning. That's really what's wrong with our school and America and a lot of other places. There's something spiritually wrong!"

"You want to be the hero our country, our *world*, needs?" Hortense almost chanted, looking straight into his mesmerizing dark eyes.

"Yes. I will make our school and our country great again. I will make our school and our world believe in themselves again."

"Our school?" I repeated, interested by the way he sort of just lumped it in with the world.

"Yes! Our *school!*" he shouted with a dazzling sincerity. "I'm beginning with our *school!*"

68

11

I told Hortense definitely *not* to do any more typing for Jason, because it was clear he was going to get himself into more and more trouble with Dean Niboff and everybody else. But she said Jason had promised he wasn't going to put any more bulletins up and that he wouldn't mention our names on anything he did, because he was very sorry we had been called down to the Dean's office. So Hortense did type up another tape he made, and she said it was really mainly because it would help her to work out her own analysis of Jason. She said it was clear nobody had really taken the time to look into the heart and soul of this boy and understand exactly what made him tick. She really thought now we *could* help him some, and she said I ought to know more than anyone that writing out one's thoughts is the very best thing there is for self-therapy. She thought maybe ours was the therapy he needed—because apart from thinking he was Icarus, he made a lot of sense.

Anyway, everything was going along fine, and once in a while we'd meet Jason in the school halls and he'd usually say he was feeling very optimistic about things and that he thought of us a great deal and how lucky he was to have friends like me and Hortense. He was bringing Darwin to school with him every day, and Darwin would usually sit outside the Vinnis Street entrance to the school, and sometimes Hortense and I would open the door and toss him a peanut butter sandwich or an Oreo cookie. Jason would check on him between classes, and I had to admit that huge black dog was getting to be almost cute. A few times Jason even cajoled a teacher to let the dog sit in class with him, but that usually drew loud comments from the other kids, and Jason would be told to put Darwin back outside. To tell you the truth, Hortense and I were both very proud to be seen with Jason. We sure made an interesting-looking trio.

In the halls, Jason always leaned against something when he talked, and his eyes were focused on us like we were the most important people in the world to him. I guess we *were* the only ones in his life, except for Darwin and Aunt Mo'. Of course, a lot of the Hormone High kids laughed behind our backs, but most of them just didn't want to have anything to do with Jason Rohr. And Dean Niboff was especially mean-looking anytime he had to pass Jason and us. Every time something nasty was done to Jason, it always seemed to be June Peckernaw and Rocky Funicelli at the bottom of it. One time Jason was in Miss Rogman's typing class, and while Jason was busy at the typewriter, June Peckernaw had the kids in his row pass up a Valentine's Day card saying TO MISS ROGMAN FROM JASON ROHR. The class

70

started laughing so hard, Jason finally looked up just as Miss Rogman was given the card from the kid in the first seat, who really didn't know where it had come from. Now Miss Rogman is a good sport, so when she got the card and read the envelope, she announced very good-naturedly and loudly for the whole class to hear, "Why, thank you, Jason!" But then she opened the card, and inside was a picture of Cupid sticking an arrow into a Kewpie doll in an embarrassing place—and someone had printed: HAPPY VALENTINE'S DAY, MISS ROGMAN. YOU'RE MY FAVORITE VALENTINE BUT YOU'RE GOING BALD. GET A WIG AND WE'LL GET IT ON! LOVE, JASON ROHR. Of course, Miss Rogman knew Jason hadn't sent her the card. But we heard that Miss Rogman looked ready to cry, because she *is* going a little bald. Then a few days later June and Rocky sent a box of fudge to Dean Niboff with a note saying LET BYGONES BE BYGONES. SINCERELY, JASON ROHR. The Dean wouldn't touch it, but his secretary ate some and it was clear to her the fudge had been made with Ex-Lax.

Then this one Tuesday in fourth-period lunch Hortense and I were just sitting around when Jason walked in. The school cafeteria at Hormone High looks very much like a prison dining room. There's about fifty long wooden tables with enough chairs to seat about eight hundred kids. And the whole thing looks like at any moment George Raft is going to file in, sit down, take one look at the food, and start banging a metal cup on the table causing a riot in which all the prisoners scream, "Alka-Seltzer! Alka-Seltzer!" You have your choice of getting on the hot-food line or the cold-food line, and if you get on the cold-food line, you go through and select old-looking ham-and-cheese sandwiches, an apple or an orange, an ice-cream pop, and sometimes if they really want to drive your palate crazy,

71

they'll have some sort of bread pudding with raisins or garbanzo beans in it. The hot-food line is a different place, where you grab your tray and shove it along on these long metal tubes and you can barely see the workers because they're behind steam tables. It's like Dante's version of Purgatory, and some of the morsels floating around in these aluminum trays look like everything from French fried worms to chicken steaks from a hostile galaxy. What you can see of the workers themselves is basically their white uniforms, and they're usually at least seventy-three years old and weigh over two hundred and fifty pounds apiece.

So by the time Jason joined us, most of the other eight hundred Hormone High teenage cannibals were devouring their brown bags of Gummy Bears, pickled eggs, pretzels, and meatball heroes from Mazzarelli's Market. Hortense and I were sipping containers of milk and watching our Dixie cups of soy-bean-violated vanilla ice cream grow soft.

"Hi." Jason smiled, dropping his books on the table right next to us.

"Hi," we said.

"We're really cooking today," Jason laughed. Then we saw he wasn't going to sit down with us.

Instead, under his left arm was a massive quantity of photocopied sheets, and he began passing them out to the kids at the next table.

"*Uh-oh,*" I said to Hortense.

"Better check it out," Hortense ordered.

I went to Jason, who was already starting on another table, plunking down a dozen copies of his latest bulletin. He told the kids to pass them along.

"What are you doing?" I asked Jason discreetly.

"I've got to get the word out!" Jason beamed.

"You said you weren't going to do any more bulletins."

"Right, no more bulletins in the halls!"

"But you're handing them out."

"I never said I wasn't going to distribute them. And I didn't put your *names* on them!"

I grabbed a couple of the bulletings and went straight back to Hortense, who was now looking very concerned because Jason was beginning to attract attention. At least the few hundred kids at our end of the lunchroom began to read what was on the paper.

"Oh, no," Hortense moaned, her eyes wide as Frisbees as she skimmed a copy:

ARISTOTLE KNEW HOW TO CREATE A MEANINGFUL CURRIC-
ULUM! Dean Niboff and Principal Greenburg hide in
their offices and we know they don't care about us.
Aristotle would never have let them into his acad-
emy at the court of Phillip the Great of Macedon!
He would have tied them naked to the roof and left
them for vultures to tear limb from limb. He would
have poured hemlock down their throats.

Aristotle was a great teacher! He taught his
students things they needed to know, like how to
make war machines, catapults, and flying tubs of
hot oil to protect them from the barbarians. He
taught them the stories of Homer and mythology,
where the secrets of happiness and godliness lie.

No, everybody isn't O.K.! Aristotle and Socrates knew it. We're in hot water! Shape up or ship
out, Dean Niboff and Principal Greenburg! I will
give you one week to change your ways. Or you'll
have to answer to me and to the spirit of Aristotle.

ICARUS, a god

12

Long before Jason had distributed his bulletins to the entire lunchroom mass of seething Hormone High kids, Hortense and I could see trouble.

June Peckernaw had been laughing hysterically from the moment Jason had come into the cafeteria. It was like she knew some delicious secret, and she left her table down at the end of the room just to grab one of the sheets and bring it back to Rocky Funicelli and half the football team. But there was something weird about how June and Rocky and a few of the others were laughing *before* they had even read the sheet. We just sensed they had done something to hurt Jason, but we couldn't figure out what. Then Mr. Rickenbacker, who was the duty teacher for the period, grabbed a bulletin and asked Jason if he'd gotten permission to hand out such a thing. And the kids were beginning to get out of hand. Some of them started banging spoons and laughing, others were standing up making believe they were great orators reading selections from the bulletin.

By the time Hortense and I got really moving, the whole cafeteria was in an uproar. We reached Jason before he got as far as June Peckernaw and Rocky Funicelli's table. But Rocky was already yelling to Jason, "Hey, loony bird; you need a few more over here! Hey, nutty buddy! And *how's your little doggie?*"

"Jason, I think we should get out of here," we told him.

"Let's go," I urged.

"Why?" Jason asked, still excited. He passed out more copies of his bulletin to a table of freshmen, who looked bewildered.

"Because I don't think they're going to understand what you're doing," Hortense chimed in.

"And I think we'd better check on Darwin," I said, because Rocky's remark had made me uneasy.

By now more kids were banging silverware and trays on the table, and Mr. Rickenbacker had already sent for help. In another minute Dean Niboff was walking very swiftly from the entrance doors at one end of the cafeteria right by the smoking steam tables, and he had a few backup teachers, including a couple of hefty gym teachers and one social studies teacher who looked just like "The Hulk."

"They're coming," Hortense told Jason, pulling on his arm.

"Who?"

It was too late.

In a moment Dean Niboff and his posse were standing smack in front of Jason.

"What do you think you're doing?" Dean Niboff asked him.

"Just spreading the word."

"Did you receive permission to do this, Mr. Rohr?" Dean Niboff asked, reaching out, picking up one of the bulletins, and checking it had been signed "Icarus, a god." I could tell he got the gist of the whole thing very quickly.

"If you don't mind coming with us, Mr. Rohr, we have a couple of things we'd like to talk to you about."

"I'll be with you in a few minutes," Jason said, smiling.

"Oh, not in a few minutes, Mr. Rohr, I mean immediately."

"No. You see, I've still got a few hundred kids here I gotta hand these things out to, you know, freedom of speech and all that sort of stuff, but I'll be right with you."

"Come with us, Mr. Rohr, or we'll drag you out of this cafeteria."

"No, you wouldn't do that," Jason warned.

Dean Niboff reached out to grab the remaining pile of bulletins in Jason's arms, and we knew *that* was a mistake. We saw anger flash in Jason's eyes, and we were afraid he might haul off and punch the Dean. Instead, he just held on to his papers and turned quickly, a motion that shoved the Dean onto one of the cafeteria chairs. The Dean lost his balance and went over backward onto the floor. As the Dean went down, June Peckernaw and Rocky Funicelli let out a scream that was picked up by the rest of the football team and the entire cafeteria. There was a tremendous round of cheers and whistling and the trays began to bang again, spoons started to fly through the air.

Hortense and I were pushed out of the way by Mr. Sweeney and Mr. Trella, the gym teachers, as they stepped in and grabbed Jason, dragging him off to one of the exit doors. As they pulled him by June Peckernaw and the football table, Rocky yelled out to Jason loud and clear: *"Your pooch sure has a great appetite!"* June and the others almost passed out laughing at the remark, and I began to feel sick.

"Get your hands off me," Jason yelled.

They only tightened their grip.

Suddenly, he shook his body and the teachers went flying. Jason took his remaining armful of bulletins and threw them high into the air so they came down like giant confetti and fell over the heads and tables of the kids in the far corner of the cafeteria. In another moment Mr. Rickenbacker and the two gym teachers, together with "The Hulk," had closed in on Jason, and Jason was yelling, "Hands off me, just hands off me. I'll go where you want, *just hands off me!*" And his voice echoed as they surrounded him, yanking him up one of the stairwells. "There's freedom of speech, you know! Freedom of speech!" were the last words we could hear as the doors closed.

We wanted to go right after them all and try to help Jason, but we knew that would be useless. We raced to a rear stairwell and went up the stairs three at a time. We hit the first floor near the main office and ran as fast as we could to the Vinnis Street exit. With a shove on the metal bar door handle, we were outside on the entrance steps— but there was no Darwin. All we saw was, on the top step, a crumpled sheet of waxed paper with what looked like a half-eaten glob of chopped meat that had been sprinkled with a gray powder.

"They've poisoned him!" Hortense cried.

I felt helpless and awful.

Then we heard the plaintive, barely audible whine. There was Darwin.

The animal lay on the ground beneath a rhododendron bush, his body shaking, nearly convulsive with his dying sounds and poor dumbfounded eyes looking at us.

Hortense screamed for me to find Jason—make Dean Niboff and his henchmen let Jason go—but I knew there wasn't time for that!

"Help me," I yelled, bending down, putting my arms around Darwin's huge shoulders. I strained and managed to lift the front part of him off the ground. "We've got to get him to a vet!"

Hortense grabbed Darwin's lower half, and together we heaved and slid all hundred and forty pounds of him along the grass toward the curb. A few of the early-duty teachers were leaving, and one of them, Mr. Prehn, a very nice history teacher who lives with his mother up on Gorham Hill, stopped his car. He got very flustered, wanting to know what had happened.

"They poisoned our dog!" was all Hortense kept shouting, filled with anger. "Some kids poisoned our dog!"

Mr. Prehn didn't really know exactly what she was talking about, but he got out to help. He grabbed an old blanket out of the trunk of his car and helped us slide the still-whining dog onto it, and the three of us used it like a sling to lug Darwin over and into his blue Toyota.

"What can we do? What can we do?" Mr. Prehn kept muttering.

"*Casa de Pets!*" I screamed at him "Casa de Pets on Nicola Avenue! He needs a vet! A vet!"

In a moment we were peeling rubber away from the school. Mr. Prehn was behind the wheel flooring the accelerator like a pro—I was in the death seat next to him, and Hortense sat in the back with Darwin's head resting on her lap. The dog was looking at us so gratefully now, his body still shaking—but his low whine now seemed less frightened, almost a purr.

13

Hortense and I were very impressed at the way the head veterinarian, Dr. Montez, handled the emergency at Casa de Pets. I once had a friend who brought a sick cat there, and I had always considered it the St. Elsewhere of animaldom—but they had redone the place on the inside and a lot of young nurses and staff, including Dr. Montez himself, jumped right into our case the moment we slung Darwin in the front door. Dr. Montez took one look and in a flash had this one orderly rush the dog into one of the rear examining rooms and lay him out on an aluminum table. They were getting a rather large stomach pump down into him before a nurse told us we'd have to get out and stay in the waiting room to fill out forms. I made Hortense say the dog was hers and give her address, because her parents wouldn't be as shocked to find they suddenly had a Great Dane in surgery. But the whole place was great—they

79

didn't even want to know if we had Animal Blue Cross or anything like that—all they did was get the basic information, and within less than an hour Dr. Montez had sent out word Darwin would live—but they'd have to keep him there at least overnight.

Hortense and I went thankfully out of Casa de Pets and hurried back to school to look for Jason. I told her he might probably only end up with spending a little time in the Dean's office or one of the detention areas and then at worst they might call Aunt Mo' and have her come down for a little conference, but that everything would eventually blow over. I knew Jason'd be checking for Darwin if they let him.

We ran all the way back to Hormone High, went straight up, and checked out Dean Niboff's office, but Jason wasn't there. Then we checked with Mrs. Reilland in the front office, but she said she didn't know what had happened to anybody. We looked a couple of other places in school and finally decided they must have sent him home.

Hortense and I both thought it'd be a good idea to call Aunt Mo', and she said Jason wasn't home yet—but we told her what had happened to Darwin and that he was going to be okay and she should tell Jason. We didn't tell her about Jason's trouble at school, because we hoped that had passed by now. Then we hung around in the front of the school on Vinnis Street, watching and waiting just in case they had Jason inside and were going to let him go home late. But after they closed the school down at four, I finally suggested we get on the 112 bus and ride it to Milden Avenue so we could go straight to Jason's house and wait for him there.

There weren't very many kids on the bus by this time, because all of them had either cut school earlier or left at three o'clock sharp. But there were mainly a lot of people starting to come home from work and they were busy reading the headlines that blasted out at us, announcing things like "Dive-Bombing Birds Frighten Nuns at Picnic" and "Ill-Fated Wedding of Two Television Stars!"

It was after four-thirty by the time we got to the ramshackle dark-brown house at the end of Milden Avenue. The late-afternoon shadows had started to form and as we went up the driveway the place looked even more ghastly. The broken windows were still covered with Glad Wrap or some other kind of cellophane that flapped in the wind, but this time there was no smiling Jason standing at the missing front door; instead there was only Aunt Mo' sitting on the first step of the spiral staircase. The dogs weren't barking, and Aunt Mo' looked very, very sad. She simply gazed at us like a living mummy until we went up closer onto the porch steps.

"They *took* him," she said helplessly.

We could hear a great cracking in her voice.

"They took Jason?" I asked in shock. *"Where?"*

"They took him away. They're putting him away again," she said, bursting into tears. At this point a blast of the giant dogs barking came from the backyard.

"They always take him away," she said, tears still rolling down her face. But it was very strange, because though her eyes were crying, her face wasn't. Her face stayed wrinkled but stolid. Sadness for her seemed so far inside, she looked for a moment like one of the ancient Indian women in her Guatemalan paintings.

"What do you mean, *they took him away?"* Hortense wanted to know.

"They put him back in the sanitarium."

"What sanitarium?"

81

"I don't know . . ." Aunt Mo' muttered.

"How can you *not* know?"

"It's that one on the top of the hill. The Sea Vista or something," she said. "That's where I always go visit him when they put him away."

"How often do they put him away?" I wanted to know.

"He's never lasted in any school more than a few months, except one time when he was ten. He lasted almost a year that time. They said he went out of control today. Two policemen brought him here and they told me he'd been acting crazy again at school. They showed me the papers, the things he was writing. . . . I told them there's nothing wrong with him. He's a wonderful boy. He's so creative, he's a genius. But nobody understands him. I showed them the wings and told Jason straightaway what had happened to Darwin and how you said he was okay at Casa de Pets."

"*What wings?*" I wanted to know.

"The ones in the garage. Didn't he ever show you his wings in the garage?"

"No," I said. "Could we see them?"

"They're beautiful. He's very talented, my nephew. Very fine and such a sweet boy to me . . ."

"Shut up! Shut up!" she began to yell at the dogs. "I gotta let it soak! Shut up back there! I'm mixing the cheese and bread," she explained to us.

But the dogs didn't stop. They went on and on as Aunt Mo' lifted herself up with her cane. We helped her down the porch steps and around the side of the house. She was still wearing her old army pants and bulky ripped blue sweater, and I caught a whiff of that strange, fermented odor about her as though she'd just been exhumed from an ancient grave.

The garage, with all its sides sinking, was in even worse shape than the house.

"In there," she said, pointing with her cane.

We moved ahead of her to the huge worn and rotting doors. I lifted a rusty hook and swung the left half door open. Inside several mice went scurrying as light flew in from the setting sun. We were amazed to see a hang glider sitting in the center of the dirt floor.

"He's been making it from a home kit, and puttin' different things on it that he could find around the junk shops," Aunt Mo' offered proudly, drying her eyes.

The glider looked more like a junky homemade sort of thing that one really wouldn't want to do any serious sky gliding in. There were some parts of it that hadn't been covered with canvas yet, with only metal tubing protruding.

"Jason's always loved flying, you know," Aunt Mo' said.

"Oh, we know," I said.

"He was goin' to take the lawn-mower motor and hook up some sort of propeller so he could turn it into one of those power-driven kinds of things," Aunt Mo' added.

In the stark final rays of sunlight, her face looked like that of a very old Indian. With the chorus of barking dogs in our ears, we walked around the entire width of the wingspan. There were several points where a sort of nuts-and-bolts assembly looked like it would allow the glider to fold up and be portable, though now it was stretched out in all its impressive width. One of the last rays of sunlight shot through a knothole and struck the front center of the glider. A touch of sparkling pure white caught my eye, and I moved closer to see that Jason had begun to attach several long white feathers to the leading edge of the wing. The feathers seemed to be more decoration than anything, but it certainly gave us pause. *Icarus! Icarus, flying to the sun!*

Before we left, we helped Aunt Mo' feed the herd of dogs and told her not to worry about Darwin or Jason— that we'd check on him, make sure everything would be all right. Of course, we hadn't the faintest idea how we were going to do any of it, but Aunt Mo' just looked like she needed a little moral support.

By six-fifteen we had walked back up Milden Avenue, stopped at a 7 Eleven, and looked up the number for the Sea Vista Sanitarium for the Young. We called the number, and what sounded like some sort of receptionist told us that indeed a Mr. J. Rohr had been admitted to their hospital, but that he would not be receiving phone calls or visits except from his immediate family. We told the nurse that we were friends from school, and she said there was nothing she could do, that it would be best if we contacted Mr. Rohr's family because the hospital was not permitted to give out information. Then she hung up on us, and we just stood there a long while near the Ms. Pac-Man and Centipede machines feeling bad.

The next morning Hortense and I went to school. On the way we called Casa de Pets, and they told us Darwin was recovering nicely but would need a week of observation and a lot of special dog vitamins. And we must have called the sanitarium at least a dozen times during the next three days. We tried a few times very late at night, thinking there might be someone on the night shift who would be nicer, willing to talk to us and give us news about Jason. Twice we stopped by his house on Milden Avenue, and Aunt Mo' hadn't heard anything from him either. She said

84

she'd called a couple of times, but that he couldn't talk to anyone because he had been sedated and was going through a battery of routine medical examinations before a psychiatrist would be assigned to him. They told her it was best if her first visit would be in a month.

Friday afternoon a messenger came up from the main office with a pass for me and interrupted our history class. Hortense watched me as I left the room. The messenger gave me the pass and said that my grandmother was waiting for me outside the main office. I didn't know what on earth was going on. Neither of my grandmothers could come down to school unless they had gotten themselves out of their graves, so I was shocked. What I found was Aunt Mo' waiting outside Room 101 near the bulletin board. She had gone into the main office and had Mrs. Reilland issue the pass for me saying it was an emergency.

"Gotta talk to ya alone," Aunt Mo' said, with everybody in the main office leaning out the door looking at what must have appeared to be the Hickey family bag lady. And indeed, she *was* carrying a shopping bag that looked like it weighed a ton.

"You heard from Jason?" I asked.

"Yes," she smiled. "He called last night, said he managed to sneak into the nurses' station and dial before they caught him."

"How is he?"

"He wants you to bring him this," she whispered.

"What? What is it?"

"A car jack."

"*A car jack?*" I repeated, slightly puzzled. "What does he want with a car jack?" I asked.

"I don't know—he just wants you to bring it to him."

"But Hortense and I called and they said we can't. Only

85

somebody from the immediate family can go see him. Why don't *you* bring it to him?"

"They'd search me," Aunt Mo explained. "They don't let anybody walk into a nuthouse with a car jack."

"But how are *we* supposed to get it to him?" I wanted to know.

"He said you'd figure out a way!"

She handed me the shopping bag and it clunked on the floor. Then she caned her way out the front exit and was gone.

I had all I could do to carry the thing, and I checked the bag out in the first-floor boys' room. Sure enough, it did have a car jack in it! The kind where you turn a crank and it expands real slowly so it can lift a heavy car.

The bell rang and I caught up with Hortense in the *Bird's Eye Gazette* room. Needless to say, she was dying to know what was up. When I told her, she was more discombobulated than I was. The reason Hortense was more freaked than me was because I had read a lot more in books about the paths heroes have to take. I know all those things about how a real hero needs an amulet or magic object to fight against the dragon forces. There is a part in every hero's life where they need some sort of supernatural aid, and this just seemed to be fitting right into that part of everything that we knew about Jason. In almost every story I ever read about a hero, there's always a little old crone or withered man who supplies a gift to help the hero get to where he's got to go. But I must admit I never read anywhere in literature where the supernatural aid provided by a spiritual guide turned out to be a *car jack*. Hortense once told me that among the American Indians in the Southwest, she read in one of her shrink books, the favorite kind of old lady who bails out the hero in dream interpretations is usually someone called the spider woman. She's a grandmotherly little dame who lives underground, and she comes digging her way up every time the hero gets in trouble. Hortense said according to these Indians, the spider woman always gives the hero a feather or other token of the alien gods. She tells him to do things like put his feet down on pollen and to rub pollen in his hands and his hair, and then the hero will have the protecting power of Destiny. Hortense said all the shrink books say it's like a subconscious wish-fulfillment dream that the piece of paradise will come eventually as a reward for the hero. And that some psychiatrists think it's only some dream about the safety of the mother's womb.

Now this is where our story gets really strange, and I'm sorry, but everything I have written down has been true. In fact everything in this book is absolutely true. It just *sounds* nuts. We left early on the 112 bus to check out the Sea Vista Sanitarium for the Young, and it turned out just to be one of the sections of a whole group of buildings on top of Manor Hill Road. There's this sort of one huge hilltop on Staten Island that you have to transfer from the 112 bus to the 111 bus to get to. And this whole complex of buildings and vast acreage is called Sea Vista Hospital. When you go in the main gate, there is a guard and guardhouse, but a very wide gate and two lanes for traffic. There's a great big building way at the far end that sometimes the 111 bus used to have to take a detour near for over a year when they were fixing Manor Hill Road. And we remembered that one building used to be used as a TB hospital but then changed into a regular hospital for old people. And then on the other side of the road was another set of buildings that is still the Staten Island poorhouse. But we had never known that there was a special nuthouse for kids up there!

We met some tired, flat-footed, garrulous nurse who was walking along from the bus stop heading from the main gate, and she was the one who pointed out the various buildings and told us where the old TB patients had been and where the poor people were, and when I asked her where they kept the crazy teenagers, she said that they processed them in the main building but then moved them into another building that in the old days used to be used exclusively for communicative diseases. She also said they did have some children who were as young as five or six years old who were bonkers, too, that stayed there. Anyway, this building, the sanitarium part of the poorhouse complex, was very small. It was only one long single-story building that was about a thousand feet from the main gate off to the left and set back in a cluster of trees. The whole hospital and poorhouse were set in a lot of greenery that wasn't terribly well landscaped, but it was nevertheless sort of pretty and bucolic, and the only thing really weird about the whole place was what you'd see if you took the bus in the wintertime and went by: There were a lot of steam pipes underground running from building to building, so there would be snow over everything but pockets of steam shooting up here and there. It made the landscape very weird. Also there were a lot of cats that had gone wild. They just lived all over the grounds, and even in the wintertime you could see them jumping from steam hole to steam hole to keep warm and dip up rats and mice that were in the ivy. So we're talking very strange here. Even without snow it was almost like another planet. And the only other thing I really knew about it was from one of the dieticians, who used to be a friend of an aunt of mine; she told me that the huge vats that they made hot oatmeal and onion soup in became tremendous containers for thousands of cockroaches to play and snack in at night.

Anyway, we headed for the place where we thought Jason would be, but it wasn't easy carrying the shopping bag with the car jack in it. I'd seen when we had gone by the entrance that the guard on duty at the gatehouse looked about as old and jolly as Santa Claus. Also we weren't the only civilians walking on this long green stretch between the main road and the gate, because it was also a horse path, and sometimes kids and guys would come trotting by on these old horses they rent from a stable over near Clove Lake. By the time we reached the roadway that was the actual entrance to Sea Vista, the Santa Claus-looking guard was busy checking three cars in a row and giving them visitors' passes, so he didn't even notice us walk right around the edge of the fence and half run, half hobble with the heavy jack toward the long one-story building in the far group of trees. I had sized the gate man up as being one of those kinds of guys we could tell we were out picking chestnuts or something and he'd believe us. Then, as we got nearer to this weird low building, there were more steam pipes and valves sticking out of the ground, and a hisssssssssssing coming out of some of them. We must have seen at least ten or twenty cats running this way and that. And they all looked extra strong and fat, with a double thick layer of fur, which I think is what happens to cats that are left to take care of themselves.

When we reached the trees, we stopped to check out the main entrance of this little building. It was just a plain pair of double doors with a lot of glass in them, and you could see a rather mean-looking nurse sitting behind a desk right as you'd go in. She looked like a very large albino vulture that would probably fly at us in a moment and call the Santa Claus guard to come get us. So we decided to bypass her and start going around the back side of the building. Since all the windows were just about at my eye level, I began peeking into a lot of them—even though they all had bars on them. The first few rooms looked like the ordinary kind of hospital room where they keep supplies and some blood centrifuge machines and those cabinets with lots of gauzes and needles if they had to give some kid a quick sedative. A few of the other windows had some little kids playing with blocks and things. A few didn't really look too happy, but a lot of them looked pretty normal. And all the time I was checking out these windows, Hortense was getting very nervous, and I told her she should just consider this a field trip for a very nifty psychology course.

Then we got really lucky, because I heard someone going, "Spttt! Spttt!" and I looked at this next open window and there was Jason, with his arms protruding through the bars and making the *spttt* sound.

Hortense and I ran to him.

"I knew you'd come," he said. "*I knew you'd come.*"

"Listen, we've gotta get you out of here," I said.

"Are you all right?" Hortense wanted to know.

"Fine," Jason whispered. "All they did so far was give me an electroencephalogram and put me on a treadmill. But some of the doctors talked to me and said they needed to move me soon to a bigger nuthouse."

"Did they say how long you'd have to stay in?" I whispered as low as can be.

"I'm *not* staying," Jason said.

"But maybe they could help you," Hortense suggested

90

gently. "Maybe a little psychoanalysis wouldn't hurt you—would only make you smarter."

"No," Jason said with a strong tone of fear. "They'd give me a brain operation or drugs to destroy my mind. Did you bring the jack?"

"Yeah."

"Give it to me," Jason said, reaching his hands farther out through the bars.

I took the gizmo from the shopping bag and passed it up to him. It slid easily through the bars. Then I passed him this separate metal crank that went with it.

He grabbed the jack and crank, quickly hid them under his bed, and moved back to the window. Then he reached out and took Hortense's right hand and my left. Hortense and I had to practically stand on tiptoes and lean against the brick building in order for him to reach far enough. I saw a couple of old milk crates with rusted metal bottoms nearby, but since I'm over six inches taller than Hortense I wasn't too anxious to get one for her to stand on. As it was I could see Jason was half naked in a white hospital gown that was only long enough to reach the tops of his legs, and he let it hang practically open in the front with just this white cloth belt that was supposed to hold it closed if a patient wrapped it around right and stayed in bed, I suppose. As it was I knew Hortense could see most of Jason's bare chest and I got to behold his bellybutton. I mean, he *could* have been more modest and kept the gown closed, and even though his mind was probably on more celestial and dynamic matters, still I didn't like Hortense having to look at so much of his flesh. And I know that as stupid as this sounds, the real reason I didn't want Hortense to see any more of Jason was that I was jealous. Jason did have the body of a young Greek god, if you like that sort of thing. My body compared to his was more like a young Australian emu, and I really disliked myself for envying anything about poor Jason in his present predicament.

He whispered urgently as he held our hands, his powerful eyes shooting down at us from behind the bars.

"Is Darwin O.K.?"

"Yes," Hortense whispered back.

"He's doing fine at Casa de Pets," I added. "They really like him down there. We just called them again before coming here."

Jason's eyes shone. "You see, you two are my greatest friends, and I want to see you up among the heavens with me! Because I really think you two are of another time as well! Harry, I think you are Euripides, the great Greek writer. And Hortense, I think you're the Delphic Oracle! I think you two have been reincarnated, just like me. When I first saw you, I just knew that being with you would concentrate new levels of strength in me and make me smarter than I ever was. Just having you two around to talk to and tell things to has given me the strength I need. And now if you will accept the roles that are truly yours, we could really have a chance of saving—the *world!* That's what I wanted to tell you. I need your help now. I need more and more from you both. I know there's going to be a lot of trouble ahead, and unless you two are by my side, I'm not going to stand a chance. I need you to listen to *all* my ideas and then put them inside your heads and think about them and *dream* about them."

Hortense suddenly fixed him with a stare of her own. "Why were you making wings in your garage?" she wanted to know.

"I don't know," he finally said.

92

"Is it just some kind of instinct?" Hortense pursued.

"Yes, that's what it is," Jason said thoughtfully. "I just think I'll need them. Nobody wants to let me leave. Something from my father thousands of years ago is having me make the wings. My father told me once in a vision that a god-boy is still to come—that the two or three thousand years we've waited since Mount Olympus is really only a moment in infinity. It was foretold that someday a god-boy would come! And that god-boy is me! I am Icarus, and everything I do and say now will have an effect on so many students and PTA groups and people everywhere that I will change the world. I'm here to signal the move of the West to the front of power. Now we're all blind! Economics is blind! Politics is blind! The Spirit is blind! We're lost and we've lost our heroes. Icarus needed harmony. That's what genius is—a drive toward harmony. Icarus was a builder, a genius. A starting point! And I AM THAT STARTING POINT!!!!"

Jason still held onto our hands, but we were all getting very uncomfortable. Jason could see it was a real strain for Hortense.

"Pull over a couple of the milk crates," he ordered me.

I turned and looked back at the weird landscape with the little areas of steam escaping from the ground and the tough-looking cats stalking mice and squirrels. I saw a couple of fairly sturdy crates and pulled them over, but I really didn't like Hortense getting up any higher and having to look at so much of Jason's body. I even thought about speaking up and telling Jason to close his hospital gown before he caught cold. But I decided that would be bringing too much attention to the matter.

I helped Hortense up onto her crate, and I could tell that she was embarrassed, too. But Jason continued in an urgent whisper. "Here at the hospital I've had even deeper thoughts, and you've both been in so many of them. . . ."

"We're very glad," I muttered.

"And precisely what have some of these 'deeper thoughts' been?" asked Hortense.

Jason glared at her. "I realized what true savages we are . . . the human animal. We are savage and saint together! In this prison I asked myself if I was the one who was frozen. Perhaps it *is* me who is wrong. Hortense, it was a few things you said to me that made me question myself for a short terrible time. In this nightmare I didn't know if I was on earth or in a dream. And last night, alone— here at the window in the moonlight—I stood alone at the bars and I thought of *you*. . . ."

"Of me?" Hortense insisted on being specific.

"Yes!"

"You mean me *and* Harry?"

"No," Jason corrected. "During this time I'm trying to tell you about it was only *you*, Hortense. I had known days before that Harry was the reincarnation of Euripides, the writer. It was you, Hortense, who was the last piece of the puzzle for me until the Great Demon came into my room and tried to destroy me."

"The Great Demon?" Hortense asked in a sort of whispered gulp.

"Yes," Jason said. "He, the demon, had been in my room setting up golden and scarlet barricades of delusion and horror. He was here as Fear itself. And the only way I could contend with this adversary was by thinking of you."

"Why her?" I wanted to know, and I really didn't like the way Hortense had been so singled out. I mean, I was beginning to feel as though I wasn't even there.

"Don't be infantile," Hortense said to me, without even taking her eyes off Jason.

I'm not infantile, I wanted to bray at her.

"When I realized you were the reincarnation of the Delphic Oracle," Jason went on, mainly to Hortense but tossing me a token glance here and there, "well, it was then I knew you would have all the answers I would need to fight the demon. Here, in this spot, in the moonlight with the beast in my room, I knew you would be the one to let me rise above the mortal condition imposed on me at my birth."

Suddenly there was a tremendous clanking sound as though some out-of-tune calliope was rolling down the center hallway. Hortense and I ducked as this contraption, containing a couple dozen steel trays of food, halted nearly outside Jason's doorway.

"You'd better go," Jason said. "The nurse'll be in here in a minute with my dinner. . . ."

"Are they feeding you good?" Hortense wanted to know.

"They have chemicals in it," Jason said. "But don't worry about me. With the tire jack I'll be out tonight."

"How?" I wanted to know.

"I can wedge it between the bars and it'll split them apart," Jason explained, but I could see his eyes were again more powerfully focused on Hortense, and his hospital gown was practically blowing in the breeze.

"And you truly believe I am the Delphic Oracle alive again," Hortense just had to pursue. "You think I am the ancient woman who sat among the volcanic rocks at Delphi and knew the answers to all questions?"

I just couldn't believe how serious Hortense sounded. I mean, she looked really mesmerized, and if she really wanted to help Jason she'd better help me get the crates away from his window, and we'd both better get out of there so no one would know there'd been a delivery to a specific nuthouse window. I got down off my milk crate and turned my back on them for just a moment while I carried it back to where I got it. I mean, I never was out of earshot, and I heard Jason's answer to Hortense's question:

"You are the oracle of my great mission" were the words I heard distinctly. But then there was this peculiar silence and I turned quickly back to the window to see Jason had drawn Hortense smack up to the bars and was kissing her. *Jason Rohr was kissing my girl!* And I don't mean just a little peck of friendship. He had his lips on hers like he was devouring a persimmon. Hortense finally broke the kiss, which made a sound something like a plumber's plunger. She saw me looking at them and leaped down off her crate just as a nurse's aide peeked in the doorway and yelled out, "You want milk or Kool-Aid?"

"Milk," Jason yelled over his shoulder without even turning around to her. She went back out to the contraption and began to fiddle with a tray and some ice, as Jason looked down at us.

"Get out of here *now*! I'll call you as soon as I'm on the outside."

Hortense and I didn't wait a moment. I took the empty shopping bag with us so nobody would find it lying outside his window and get suspicious. We began to run back the way we had come along the far edge of the building—back into the grove of trees. In the middle of the trees I crunched the shopping bag and stuck it under one of the steam pipes. Then, when we got closer to the gate, we waited until a car came to the gatehouse so that Santa Claus was busy checking it out.

I gave a final signal, and Hortense and I dashed to the

edge of the gate. When we got there, we slowed, just strolled around it as casual as can be, making believe we were fossil hunting or had just returned some horse there. Night began to fall as we headed toward a bus and home to the safety of our own beds.

14

I didn't call Hortense to ask about the kiss until three seventeen A.M. in the middle of the night! It took me that long to figure out if I was jealous or furious about Jason laying a wet one on her at the sanitarium. Neither of us had said a word about it on the bus ride home. We had just sat there talking as innocently as possible, as though we were really interested in Jason's concept of us as reincarnations. But subconsciously, as Hortense would say, I was really burning.

"Hortense?" I said into the phone.

"Yes . . ." I heard her sleepy voice. I had obviously woken her up, and I was glad.

"Why did you let Jason kiss you?"

"What?"

I heard the noises of her rearranging the phone wire and scrambling into a more alert position.

"You heard me," I said.

"What kiss?" she asked.

"That long, lust-filled one Jason gave you through the sanitarium bars. If you've decided to become the wife of Icarus, or even his concubine, I think I have a right to know."

"That was a kiss of friendship." Hortense's voice scolded me, and I could tell she was wide-awake now.

"In a pig's pancreas it was," I told her, and braced my ears to hear her every reaction.

"You're paranoid, Harry. Go back to sleep."

"I will *not* go back to sleep!"

"Look, I'm tired. . . ."

"Why did you kiss him like that?" I demanded to know. "You're just fascinated by him, aren't you?"

"I am not."

Anyway, I cross-examined her for over twenty minutes trying to get her to admit she had fallen in love with Jason, but all she said was that *I* was the crazy one and ought to be locked up. I mean, I just wanted to know if she was getting into the romance of the whole thing. I mean, it is a pretty good line to go up to a girl and tell her she's the reincarnation of the Delphic Oracle. That'd be worth a kiss and a lot more. I just became like a broken record and demanded to know if she was in the middle of some fantasy spell and if Jason was giving her more excitement in life than I was. I told her I'd pretend to be Louis the Fourteenth or Zorro if she'd sock kisses into me like the one she gave Jason.

Well, like I told you, Hortense has always been there for me when I needed her, and she spent a long time talking to me in her sweetest, sleepiest voice until she had finally made me feel secure about the whole thing. After about an hour more I was so tired myself, she managed to convince me I hadn't even *seen* everything I had seen and that she, me, and Jason were just three friends, and that romantic passion only flowed between her and me. She even started to make me feel guilty about having had such cheap and tawdry thoughts about her, and reminded me that Jason was really a mentally disturbed pal who needed us more than ever now. In fact, she reminded me, he might have broken out already and be trying to call us because he needed our help desperately and we were keeping the phones busy. After another forty minutes we finally had a good laugh. We weren't on much more than another ten minutes after that when I agreed to hang up, and I had no trouble going straight to sleep and having about six dozen consecutive nightmares.

By the next day I really *did* expect the phone to ring at any moment, but whenever it did it was Hortense. I told her that I thought maybe Jason had probably gotten caught breaking out. That he had probably stuck the jack between the bars and it made so much noise some nurses probably rushed in with hypodermic needles and things and knocked him out.

When we hadn't heard from him by the eleven-o'clock news that night, I figured the next thing would be that some patrol car would be pulling up in front of my house and they'd be taking me and Hortense down to the St. George precinct and booking us as accomplices in assisting a teenage maniac to escape. I could just hear the judge, and see the headline in the newspapers: "Theater Critics Slip Tire Jack to Teenage Schizo in Dramatic Sanitarium Escape Plan." Hortense even woke up in the middle of the night, remembering with a terrible dose of guilt what I had made her do. Because you see it really *was* me who talked her into it. She told me how complex schizophrenics can be. She made me read one case history about somebody called The Butcher of Anaheim. This man called Robert Stock was accused of the most shocking crime ever heard of in a small town near Disneyland. The part I remember best about it was that he ended up walking this silent corridor to the Death House. And there was this series of extraordinary things that happened because he was a very powerful, unpredictable schizophrenic. But at the end of his case history it all explained that he really was a flesh-eating demon because he never had any good friends in high school. Of course, the case study left out a lot of other important factors, but then again it was only an abstract in a journal, so we had to read between the lines.

But I knew that Hortense was becoming completely hypnotized by Jason Rohr. So it was easy to convince her to go to Sea Vista with me. And even though I was jealous later, I had to admit that I was just as drawn to Jason. There was something so blindingly perfect about his face. Anyway, Hortense is really more sophisticated than that when it comes to real love and sex. I *do* know that what we feel for each other is the closest to anything I've ever known that's true love. We're just sort of automatically a couple. And we always have been and we always will be. We'll probably be married before we ever get out of graduate school, and the only thing I know is I'm not going to let her quit her schooling just to support my writing. But there was something about the image of Jason in his hospital gown that made me feel he really *was* from another time and place and he truly had been lifted from some magical Greek island thousands of years ago and brought to the twentieth century.

The next morning Hortense and I talked, and it turned out we both had had nearly sleepless nights with visions of Jason dashing through them, flying with him, opening great golden caskets, and walking down labyrinths in which the fabulous treasures of Life were soon to be discovered.

After school the next day we checked with Aunt Mo', and she said she had heard from the sanitarium that her nephew had broken out, but she swore to us she hadn't seen him.

"My nephew might be crazy but he's not dumb," she told us. "He knows they're gonna be around here looking for him. There was some cops down the street just an hour ago."

That news scared Hortense until I told her the entire militia of Staten Island wasn't going to be called out because some disturbed teenager escaped from a budget sanitarium. I assured her that the police don't really go looking for anybody unless it's someone who goes into a movie house with a machine gun or blows up a McDonald's or a Chase Manhattan Bank.

"You don't think he'll do anything desperate?" she asked me.

"No, I don't think so," I said. But I could tell she wasn't sure. And neither was I.

15

All week Hortense and I waited to hear from Jason.

It wasn't until after the six-o'clock news on Saturday that the phone finally rang. My mother and father were busy watching the news, which had a lead story about a horrified crowd in Brooklyn seeing a woman stomped to death during a carnival ostrich race. And something about a student who killed himself in a 320-foot plunge in order to find God ahead of schedule.

The moment I answered the phone, I knew it was Jason on the other end, though he didn't speak at first. I could hear traffic in the background, so I knew wherever he was, he was at a pay phone.

"Jason, is that you?" I asked.

"Yes, Harry" came his voice, finally.

"Where *are* you?" I asked. "Hortense and I were worried. We thought you were going to call."

"I had to think things over."

"Oh."

"I want you to get over here now. I need to see you both."

"Where?" I asked.

"You know where they're building the new highway?"

"Yeah."

"Call Hortense—I'll meet you guys right now."

"But *where*? What part?"

"Walk down Glen Street to the end where the garbage dump is. Then there's a big dirt slope and a bunch of yellow earth movers and tractors and all that stuff," he specified.

"Where they've been building the overpass?"

"Yes. I'll be waiting for you," he said; then he hung up.

I called Hortense, and she answered on the first ring. Of course she said she'd meet me immediately. It couldn't have taken her more than eight minutes to get down to Victory Boulevard and Glen Street. She was already waiting under the streetlight, and we started up Glen out toward the path to the highway construction. They'd been building this highway for about three years, and the thing that was holding it up was that on the edge of our town is the major garbage dump for all of New York City, and they had to wait another year or two before there could be enough garbage to build the right bridges with what they call land-fill. I noticed Hortense was carrying her extra-large shoulder bag.

"What have you got that for?" I asked.

"I brought him salami, and we had a big piece of un-opened Monterey Jack cheese. I also threw in half a package of English muffins and a box of saltines, just in case.

104

I didn't think to bring him anything to drink," Hortense explained.

At the end of Glen Street the streetlights halted and we went into the darkness where the asphalt road turned into a dirt road, and then finally we reached the graded pathways of the construction area. When we got far enough along there was some light cast from the Con Ed electrical plant, which was right on the edge of the hill. Its hundreds of small outdoor lights cast shadows over its huge piles of coal and intricately woven high-tension wires and towers. The only reminders that we were really on earth were the mountains of garbage stretching for about a mile in front of us, where billions of sea gulls nested and squawked and in daylight could be seen to fly and circle the debris of an entire city.

Hortense and I finally got to the spot where the next in a series of overpasses was to be built. There on the ridge of a dirt slope was Jason, set against the vast shadow-ridden landscape.

He walked forward to us, put his arms around both of us, and hugged us.

"Thank you for coming," he said.

"I brought you some food to eat in case you needed it," Hortense said, handing him the salami and stuff.

"Thanks, I can use it," he said. Then he started to lead us down the dirt slope. "Come on, I'll show you where I'm hiding out."

Hortense and I began to make our way down the decline.

"Be careful," he called to us softly.

I noticed several huge yellow shapes far off to the left— the earth graders and tractors—and there were several small sheds, including one trailer that had a light on inside it.

"The watchman's in the trailer," Jason said when we reached the bottom of the grading. Then he turned and led us several hundred feet farther off the road to another small construction shed.

"*Dynamite?*" Hortense asked, shocked.

"Yeah, so they can blast through the shale. I think yesterday they blew up a part of the hill on the other side of an old cemetery. They blow up everything in order to keep the road moving straight ahead."

He led us into this other shack, which seemed to be nothing more than a storehouse for junk. There were some kerosene lamps and an electric bullhorn, and after we were inside for a while my eyes got accustomed enough to the darkness to see some wooden sawhorses they use to block roads and things like that. Jason took our hands and led us to a bed of dry hay he had piled in the corner to sleep on. It looked very much like a large condor's nest. Then, carefully, he closed the door of the shack, lit a match, and put it to a small, thick candle he had set up inside a wooden crate to help diffuse its brightness. Jason really now looked like he'd stepped out of a time tunnel. His hair was wild, and he was wearing some workman's Levi's pants and jacket, and a shirt that had very fine lined stripes in it.

"Where'd you get the clothes?" I asked.

"From the shacks at the other end near the big machine. The night watchman around here would turn me in to the police if he caught me. One time he chased me as far as the Con Ed plant, but I lost him in the coal piles."

Jason opened the bag of food, took the stuff out. He really looked happy as he took one of the English muffins and began chewing on it.

"Thanks," he said, and he put his left arm around Hor-

106

tense and gave her a big squeeze. "But I don't really have time to eat now. I've got to talk to you guys."

He put the rest of his muffin down on the crate next to the candle.

Then he puts his other arm around me.

I felt very strange sitting there in that big nest with me and Hortense both in Jason's arms, though I knew it had nothing to do with sex. It was more like we were brothers. It was like Hortense and I were his brother and sister—or maybe, *maybe* for the first time I really felt what pure friendship is—and all of this from a boy who had to be nuts. I feld so weird, but decided not to be uptight. Then Jason just lay back against the hay, and he guided us back with him, keeping his arms around us and letting us use his shoulders like big pillows. I mean, it was freaky, but not *that* freaky.

"I've been driven into the desert for a while," Jason said calmly in the candlelight. "Just like Christ and all those guys. All great changers of history get pushed out of their countries to lonely spots, where they think for a while and commune with all the other gods in the air and trees and stones. And then the day comes when their greatest visions come. When they know what they must do!"

"Do you know?" Hortense asked softly.

"Yes, now I know. I've seen the truth here near the garbage dump and this new road being built. *I know my father and mother want me to save the world.*"

"That's the root of the whole problem, isn't it?" Hortense asked calmly.

"Yes."

"But Jason, I've been doing some rereading of the Daedalus story," Hortense remarked, and I could hear her

107

voice switching into her more professional shrink tone. "You must know that the labyrinth your father built to hold the terrible Minotaur monster was a very long, mysterious, complicated place. It had numberless winding passages and turns opening one into the other, and seemed never to have a beginning or an ending. Your father built one of the greatest puzzles the world has ever known. Did you ever think that maybe now, in some way, you might even be caught in your father's own labyrinth?"

Jason didn't answer. He just hugged us closer to him.

"And I read a lot more about your father," Hortense continued very gently. "That he had *done something wrong,* and King Minos didn't like him anymore, and so the king shut him up in a tower. The king took your brilliant father who had done something wrong and took him away from you."

"But he escaped," Jason said quietly.

"Yes, your father escaped and found you waiting on the cliffs near the edge of the island. But you both had no way of going home, no way of going back where you belonged to live a normal life."

"That's when he started making the wings for us," Jason said in a whisper.

"Yes, but Jason, when you read mythology you have to think of it more as being symbolic, not history. I know that somewhere in his heart your father really did want you both to 'fly' together in some way, but I don't think it was thousands of years ago. And I don't think he really made wings!" Hortense said, now being a bit more firm with him.

Jason still held us in his arms, but moved so that he clasped our hands. I could feel a great heat in his palm, as though his hand was on fire with electric nerves.

108

"But I had a vision last night that soon I will be wounded," Jason whispered. "That there are things going on in the offices of the high and evil forces who wish to punish me further.

"Daedalus and I had many enemies in Athens and Crete and on lots of the islands as well. In this dream they ambushed me. And they ambushed you, Harry and Hortense!"

"They did?" Hortense inquired.

"But through the whole dream I knew we were going to win. I knew that in the end we would win because we were smarter than anybody else. It wasn't going to be our weapons that would save us, but it was that we would have better ideas. Eventually we would stop the whole world from blowing up. You understand that, don't you?"

"Yes," said Hortense soberly.

"I knew you'd comprehend." Jason smiled with relief.

"But what can we *really* do, Jason?" Hortense pursued.

"You've gotta get the kids at school to listen to me. I've gotta talk to them. Gotta talk to all of them. I've got so much more to say!"

"But how? And why, Jason? If you show up at the school, they're just going to call the cops and Dean Niboff and Rickenbacker and all those guys, and they're going to put you away again," I blurted.

"No, I just need to talk to them during assembly."

"You're going to talk to the assembly?" Hortense asked, her eyes popping. "They're not going to *let* you talk to the assembly. They just want to lock you up!"

"It's not a matter of them letting me," Jason said slowly, carefully. "They don't really control me anymore. Time is too short."

Jason went silent, as though some of Hortense's earlier

109

remarks were starting to knock at his subconscious. I dreaded the end of the silence, because suddenly I knew Hortense was going to go the whole distance to the truth.

"Jason," Hortense whispered with great compassion, lifting her left hand to stroke his face sweetly, lovingly, "Jason, we know what your father did to your mother . . . and to himself. Jason, *we know the truth*. . . ."

Tears began to flow from Jason's eyes, and he turned first to his left and kissed Hortense, and then I braced myself as he turned and kissed me. He just kissed me near my right earlobe, but he held his face close to mine for a long while, and then he took his arms away from us and sat forward to stare at the candle.

"You weren't there, Harry and Hortense," Jason said finally. "You weren't there to see how much my father loved me when he fitted the wings onto my shoulders. My father's face was wet with tears and his hands were trembling. He was worried about me. And my dad kissed me as I kissed you. He never really liked to show emotion, but this time he did. Then he put on *his* wings and flew off the cliff encouraging me to follow. I ran and got up enough speed, and I flew off the cliff behind him. I felt wonderful, and I knew we were the first ones in the world ever to fly! Me and my beautiful dad! And as we flew away from the cliffs toward our homeland, he kept looking back to see how I was doing, if I was managing my wings in the right way. We passed the island of Samos and Delos with all the white stone lions. I remember the whole thing. How I loved being up there with the birds, just my father and me and the great sea eagles. But I began to go crazy with joy. I wanted to fly higher, to soar upward, to reach Heaven. I saw my father's worried face below, and he yelled to me: 'STOP, MY SON! STOP!' He could see I was enraptured being in the clouds, and higher and higher I went. He tried to get up to me, to stop me, but I just laughed and sang and blew kisses down to him—until I was so high I saw the first feathers begin to fall. I don't know how it happened so quickly. One moment the sea breezes were cool, and the next there was nothing but the hot sun. The hot sun and the melting wax and my father's terrified face below me. Then, a moment later, I fluttered my arms but there were too few feathers to hold the air, and I started to fall. I fell past my poor loving father, down and down, until I was dead."

Jason was sobbing now, his body shaking, and this time it was Hortense and I who leaned forward to hold him.

16

Dear Jason,

Harry told me not to write this letter, but I really feel I have to, and I'm sorry if you're not going to like what I say in it. But I think it's only fair that I be honest with you since you've been honest with us about your great adventure and quest.

You must know by now that Harry and I really like you and you'll never lose us. We'll always be your friends—that's the first thing you've got to believe. But there's a few things I've seen, and some thoughts that go on inside me, that I wanted to tell you about. I have some ideas about you, Jason, that I've never really told you mainly because you're such a complex person and also because I never wanted to hurt you. But I think there's a lot about

you you don't really know—a lot that goes on inside your brain that's subconscious, that's still
nightmares that you are having trouble facing up
to in reality. I mean, Harry and I never met a kid
more intelligent and original. You really are one
of a kind, but I must say sometimes in spite of all
the very brave bulletins you've put out and the way
you stand up for your rights, I think you are still
very afraid of the real world. I can't lie to you
anymore because Harry and I did check the records
and found out that your father had killed your
mother when you were just six years old—and then
killed himself. We know that there was nobody around
to give you the love you needed. We know you were
moved from place to place, from institution to institution, and only sometimes did they even let
you live with your Aunt Maureen—and you know that
she's a little unusual too. There are very few people who have more than a few Great Danes. She has
just too many Great Danes to be really normal. And
that's not to say she's not a nice person. Because
it's very nice for people to like dogs. But it's
just that she is <u>very</u> different and she couldn't
give you much of a good look at life.

Harry and I are so proud that you've trusted us
more than the other kids, and that you've picked
us to be your special friends. I'm sorry that you
think Harry is Euripides, because I don't really
think he is—and I'm not the Delphic Oracle! We
went along with it as far as we could, but I guess
we have to tell you that we don't really believe
that part. What I think happened to you was that
you made a fantasy world when you were a kid because
of all the horrible things that happened. And it
must have been very hard to pull yourself out of

that fantasy world and try to stand on your own two feet as you were growing up. But you see, Jason, what I think is that when you were growing up after the terrible deaths of your mother and father, that you were living mainly within your own mind and that there was no one around to give you faith in yourself. You needed something fabulous to believe in. I think that's why when you came across that book on Daedalus and his son Icarus, you decided Daedalus would be your real father and that you would be his son. I think you wanted to be a son of a great inventor, and I know you must have been thrilled reading about Daedalus building the labyrinth thousands and thousands of years ago. At least in the myth he was a terrific father and you wanted to be his son. You wanted a father who could help you build wings that would let you fly. I think you never learned how to think the way other kids do. I think you were isolated so long in your own mind that you had to believe you were the son of this famous man. And I don't think that was a bad thing.

Jason, you see the world differently than anybody else does. You have these visions and dreams. But they are all a part of your early childhood trauma. I don't think you really do have any sense of the rules of time and space. I think there is a mystery about you. I think that Harry and I wanted to go into your world. We needed magical things to believe in again. But we weren't as honest as we should have been. We loved visiting you in your world. But I guess somewhere along the way we knew we'd have to tell you more about the world as <u>we</u> see it. Harry and I were looking for a hero and you were that hero. But we really had no right pretending we believed everything you said.

I don't expect that you're going to like everything that I'm writing in this letter, but at least when I finish it I will have been honest with you. Harry and I will have told you what we both <u>feel</u>. We want you to know that we are your friends and will be by your side as long as you need us, but we've got to be more <u>truthful</u> friends, and if we see you doing or saying something that does seem crazy, I think we've got to speak up and let you know that we don't quite see it that way. Of course, you might think we're crazy too—which is all right. I'm not sure exactly what sanity is anymore anyway.

You've been so very kind to us. We love you more than any kid we've ever met. <u>But we do think you could use a little psychiatric help</u>. We know you've had some, but maybe a little more. I've read a few books about people who have the kind of mental problem you have. In most psych books it's usually under the topic of schizophrenia. We're worried about you, and we hope you won't think we're traitors for telling you these things. What we need you to know more than anything is that we will always be your friends and will always stand up for you and defend you as being very brilliant and a very great human being. But not a <u>god</u>. We will do everything we can for you and hope that you feel our love behind each and every word of this letter.

Love,

Harry and Hortense

17

Hortense and I got up the earliest we ever had on Thursday—six A.M. We told our parents we had decided to go fishing a little before school at Willowbrook Pond.

By six-eighteen, I arrived at the corner of Glen Street and Victory, and Hortense was waiting for me. She had sealed our letter to Jason in a nice white envelope and written his name on the outside. On the back part of the envelope she had added something that really told me how dreadful she felt about having to tell Jason her true feelings about how nutty he was. She had simply written, "We really do love and respect you," and even drawn one of those silly circle faces with two dots for eyes and a little scribble for a smile.

By the time we got to the construction area, we noticed a few extra cars, and before we even got a chance to get

116

near the huge yellow dirt graders, we were stopped by a couple of workers who wanted to know where we were going. While Hortense was telling them we sometimes used this way as a shortcut to school, I noticed that two cops and what looked like a couple of construction engineers in suits were standing talking right in the area where Jason's shack was. I could see Hortense picking up on it out of the corner of her eye and knew she and I both were sure they had caught Jason.

"You're not supposed to trespass here," one of the construction workers said, sipping a coffee from a thermos.

"Yeah, you better get back on the main road," the other one grunted.

"Something wrong?" I asked, still checking the cops and guys in suits in the distance.

"Yeah," the worker with the coffee said, starting to check a gizmo on one of the smaller bulldozers. "Somebody stole dynamite."

"Dynamite?" Hortense gasped. "Stole dynamite?"

"Yeah," the second guy said, half checking our schoolbooks and faces with his eyes. I could see he didn't suspect us.

"Just can't trust anybody anymore," I said, covering the vibrato in my voice. I grabbed Hortense's arm and started marching her back toward Glen Street, but not before I saw the door to Jason's shack was wide open and the entourage of cops and guys was floating between there and the spot where the dynamite had been kept.

Hortense didn't say a word until we were all the way back to Victory Boulevard. I knew she wasn't speaking because her mind was going a mile a minute. She kept checking to make certain she hadn't dropped the letter for Jason.

"You don't think he took the dynamite, do you?" Hortense asked me finally in a whisper as we got on the 112 bus.

"No," I said weakly, and we both sat in silence just thinking for the entire bus ride.

Before eight o'clock we were already outside Hormone High, so we decided to stop at Pop's Deli across the street for some coffee and Twinkies. We had about forty-five minutes before we had to be in our homeroom, and then the bell to the usual Thursday assembly would sound at nine-ten sharp. That's when we would all march through the halls and down to the auditorium, salute the flag, and sing the national anthem. And we already knew from a story in our *Bird's Eye Gazette* that the program that morning was going to consist of the Glee Club singing "Carry Me Back to Old Virginny" and General Motors. GM was sending their usual program where they drag out a little jet engine onto the stage and start it up, which makes a big ROAAAAAAAR and the kids would all go WHOOPIE! Then we'd go back to our homerooms and wait for the bell to start our classes for the day.

"You don't think Jason's going to do anything at the assembly, do you?" Hortense said, devouring an entire Twinkie in a flash.

"No," I said. "All he said was he wanted to *talk* to the kids. Just *talk* to everybody."

"But somebody stole dynamite from that construction site."

"He's not going to blow up the school."

"Mentally disturbed kids do things like that!"

"What do you say we share some Devil Dogs and an Orange Crush?" I suggested then.

118

"Okay. I just want to give him our letter," Hortense moaned, ravaging the small-cakes rack.

"*Your* letter," I found myself correcting.

"It's from you, too," she shot at me.

"Mainly from *you*. I just signed it."

"You think we *shouldn't* try to help him."

"I didn't say that."

"You believe in him, don't you?" Hortense glared at me. "You really do think he might have been sent to earth on a mission. You just want that to be true, don't you? You want it so badly, you're beginning to confuse all his magic mumbo jumbo with reality."

"I didn't say that either," I said.

"Well, what do you believe?" Hortense wanted to know. Then she had the nerve to say, "You just shove that junk food down your throat and you're not giving me any support at all. That boy is crazy and needs help and you know it!"

"But in a way he's really a hero, too," I muttered.

Hortense took the Orange Crush out of my hand and started guzzling. She had even managed to get some crumbs into her China doll hair.

"You think he is, too, don't you?" I asked her, but she wouldn't answer.

"I know he's got the dynamite," she finally said, handing me back a nearly empty can.

"And you always call *me* paranoid."

"HARRY, IT'S NO COINCIDENCE!"

"You're getting hyper," I told her. "He's not going to blow up the auditorium because he knows *we're* going to be there. He cares about us. He needs us. He doesn't want to kill anybody. Besides, you haven't read enough novels

119

to know how heroes work. They don't just show up and lob a grenade into a crowd of pubescent nerds."

"What do they do?" Hortense glared at me.

"They go through *struggles*. *Trials*. You know, like all the things Hercules had to do!" Then I decided to really get her goat. "You love him, don't you, Hortense?" I accused her.

"You're revolting."

"I know it's only a temporary infatuation. I know you love him platonically. In fact maybe you love him just *because* he's a heroic schizoid."

"You're crazed."

"I looked at your face in the candlelight last night," I told her. "When he had his arms around us—and you looked just like this etching I saw in the front of a story about Psyche who was in the arms of her lover, Cupid."

"And when I looked at you in his other arm, I figured the two of you were going to rent a loft together," she retorted.

"You're just doing tit for tat because I'm touching on a very sensitive subject with you." I zeroed in. "But I'm only mentioning it because heroes and heroines don't go around being violent until there's no other way and they've really gone through all the trials. Jason isn't that desperate. He's prepared for bigger challenges. He wanted to talk! He still believes those lunatics at Hormone High are going to listen to him. And I want you to know that Psyche was a heroine, and even heroines go through trials and tests, and they're very smart and can solve problems. Psyche had to do something to win Cupid back because Cupid's jealous mother took him and hid him where Psyche couldn't find him."

"I really wish your mother would hide *you* somewhere," Hortense muttered, grabbing a Hershey bar with almonds,

120

and for a minute I thought she was going to eat it wrapper and all before she even paid for it.

"Psyche pleaded with the jealous mother to give Cupid back, but Cupid's mother got so angry, she grabbed Psyche by the hair and started banging her head on the ground and then kicked her around a little. Then she took like twenty-three sacks of wheat, poppy seeds, peas, lentils, and beans and mixed them all in a messy mixture around Psyche and told Psyche if she could sort them all before nighttime, then she'd give Cupid back to her," I explained.

"And, of course, she couldn't do it," Hortense snapped.

"No, she did." I grinned—Hortense looked so cute all worked up. "See, unexpected help always comes for the hero or heroine! An army of *ants* suddenly appeared and got to work with Psyche, so by nighttime everything was all sorted and she got Cupid back again. At least that's the way it was in this version I read, which I thought was a really nice happy ending. . . ."

"You really have a screw loose, Harry," Hortense said, grabbing my hand and dragging me onward to school.

18

Well, to tell you the truth, I *was* worried something would happen at assembly. Hortense and I got excuse passes from Mr. Olsen to get us out of homeroom, saying we were assigned to help direct the GM guys to set up the jet motor backstage, but actually we mainly stayed near the entrance of the auditorium while the Color Guard was getting into position and practicing so they could march in carrying the flag. The Color Guard at Hormone High was one of the truly shocking sights. Mrs. Logen was in charge of it, and because she really didn't like boy pupils she let only huge girls who looked like Amazons parade the flag into the assembly. She had them all wear short red skirts and high blue boots and white blouses. On their heads were silver two-foot-tall hats with sparkles on them, and the entire effect was always ghastly.

"What are you doing here?" Mrs. Logen asked us in a very threatening voice.

"We're doing a story on the Color Guard," I told her, and she immediately lit up.

"Oh, how lovely."

What we really were doing was running back and forth from the auditorium entrance to the school's side exit doors, where we could check to see if anybody was heading up Vinnis Street toward school. If Jason decided to come along any other direction we wouldn't see him, but I figured we had a fifty-fifty chance of spotting him where we were. Finally, the bell for the kids to pass to assembly rang, and a moment later the halls were jammed with dozens of teachers leading their classes. "ARMS' LENGTH! STAY IN LINE! I SAID IN LINE!" the teachers kept bellowing. Whistles were blowing. The school band started to play. Before we knew it, the assembly had started.

And ended.

And there had been neither hide nor hair of Jason Rohr.

By fourth-period lunch I had calmed down, and I was overjoyed Jason hadn't done anything foolish. I even had Hortense convinced she was wrong about Jason having any dynamite, and then we both got hungry and decided to risk the hot-food line, which boasted spaghetti, but when we finally got to glimpse it through the steam-table vapors, we decided it was a definite pass. Those globs of spaghetti had been arranged in little piles so they looked like botulism dumplings, and the cafeteria had hired a new cashier who looked like she had just escaped from the violent women's house of detention. Then we got on the cold-food line and decided to split a chicken-salad sandwich, and we each got a vanilla Dixie cup and a container of milk. No matter what I say about Hortense's eating habits, I really keep up with her bite for bite. We picked one of the tables in the middle to sit at—one I made sure was a good distance from the football team. I was so relieved there hadn't been any trouble that morning, I didn't even mind the fact that when we opened the sandwich, half the chicken salad had just a tinge of pink mold growing on it. We threw it into a trash can, and were perfectly happy with the ice cream and milk. Yet I still knew that Hortense would somewhere, somehow, find Jason Rohr and give him the letter, which was still in her pocketbook. We were having the nicest conversation about Jason, a very deep conversation about all the times I had read about heroes in novels and how I was going to write about them one day, and Hortense told me she had already read several case histories in which normal people had dreams about heroes and adventures. Of course, she had read cases recorded by psychoanalysts in books in which they discussed things like I had been telling her, but in the form of hallucinations and visions. We were having one of the deepest talks we'd ever had, and we even started holding hands while we were sipping our milk. We had made the mistake of picking a freshman table to sit at, and there was this one clutch of Hormone High specimens who were talking a mile a minute about how some couple they knew got wed on a rollercoaster kind of ride called Montezuma's Revenge, and about how terrific it was that a couple of senior boys had stolen a bus and driven it into the ocean. On top of that was this other girl across from us who was reading a newspaper with a headline that said, "Waitress Saves Boss from Madman's Fist" and another little item right on the front page about how the women's movement is making men into lousy lovers. The kids all read that stuff at lunch. I think it's a shame, because it's really very unscientific reporting.

But the two of us were just connecting, really *connecting,* when we first heard the voice.

At first it seemed like static. Like someone was playing with the PA system, or turning it on for some kind of announcement about a club meeting.

But then came the words:

ATTENTION! ATTENTION, ALL STUDENTS! AND TEACHERS! HELLO, TO ALL STUDENTS AND TEACHERS IN THE SCHOOL. I WANT TO TALK TO YOU! YOU TOO, DEAN NIBOFF! . . .

We were both shocked at the sound of Jason's voice on the PA—though it seemed we were the only ones who were even listening. The rest of the lunchroom just kept talking and laughing like they usually do.

HI, EVERYBODY came the voice again. I JUST WANT TO TALK TO YOU ABOUT SOME IMPORTANT THINGS. HELLO. CAN YOU HEAR ME? THIS IS ICARUS!

Hortense and I didn't know what to do, but if we had trouble hearing up to that point, there was no trouble from that moment on because by now the cafeteria had gone suddenly silent with all the kids staring at the loudspeakers. And Mr. Rickenbacker rushed out of the cafeteria.

I KNOW YOU HAVEN'T WANTED TO BELIEVE THAT I AM REALLY A GOD, BUT I AM. I AM A SPECIAL GOD WHO HAS SOMETIMES BEEN CALLED JASON ROHR. BUT I KNOW IF YOU LISTEN TO ME TODAY, YOU WON'T LAUGH AT ME OR TREAT ME THE WAY YOU DID ON OTHER OCCASIONS. . . .

"Where can he be talking from? Where's the mike?" Hortense asked me.

"There's one in the principal's office," I said, "and the main office . . . and . . ."

Jason's voice continued on the PA system, but I couldn't

understand the words, because the initial shock in the lunchroom had worn off. Now June Peckernaw, Rocky Funicelli, and most of the football team were screaming with laughter—I mean, they were making sounds like incensed chimpanzees at a zoo. Then the ever-popular tray banging echoed like a thunderous tornado spreading the entire length of the eight hundred tables. Hortense grabbed my hand and yanked me toward an exit.

The last thing I saw was Rocky Funicelli and a couple of other football guys jumping up on the tables and sprinting from one to the other heading for another exit—with June Peckernaw laughing her head off. It seemed suddenly the entire lunchroom was off to find out where Icarus was talking from.

By the time Hortense and I hit the first floor, there was a commotion of kids and teachers peering out of their classrooms. We could hear the amplified voice on the first-floor speakers still going on.

YOU SEE, WHAT YOU DON'T SEEM TO UNDERSTAND IS THAT ALTHOUGH I AM A GOD, I AM JUST A BOY TOO, AND YOU SHOULDN'T BE FRIGHTENED OF ME. I'VE BEEN SENT HERE TO HELP YOU ALL. THIS TIME I'M NOT LEAVING UNTIL I REALLY GET THINGS STRAIGHT.

We ran to the main office first, but Miss Reilland and several of the other school clerks were just sort of dazed, spinning in circles. We could see their mike to the PA was still locked behind a wire-mesh protector cage that had been installed the year before after the whole system had been ripped off.

"I hope not the principal's office," I prayed to Hortense.

She didn't answer, just started to run with me down the length of the first floor to another stairwell. By now hundreds of kids and dozens of teachers were out in the halls, looking up in amazement at the speakers. And the lunchroom crowd was beginning to come out into the halls from several other stairwells.

As we ran up to the second floor, the voice boomed from a speaker:

THE TROUBLE WITH MOST OF YOU IS THAT YOU'RE TRAPPED BEHIND THE BRICK WALLS OF YOUR MINDS! THOSE WALLS WERE MADE BY THE PLASTIC SAD VOICES YOU HEAR ALL AROUND YOU! VOICES OF HATE AND DESPAIR. VOICES OF NEGLECT! I'VE COME TO PULL YOU OUT FROM THOSE WALLS!

We arrived on the second floor at a point where the girls' gym class was beginning to flow out, listening and giggling about the voice on the PA. We had to run completely around the second-floor hallway to get to Principal Greenburg's office, but there was only his secretary and one clerk standing helplessly next to an unmanned microphone.

"Where is he talking from?" the clerk asked, as though we should know.

We just shrugged and began frantically running down the hall again, but we didn't know where we were going.

"Are those the only two mikes that plug into the PA?" Hortense asked me.

"There's got to be another," I puffed, "but *where?*"

The voice continued as we were pushed and shoved by kids madly scurrying in the hall.

I CAN HEAR YOU LOOKING FOR ME AND THAT MAKES ME VERY HAPPY. I WANT YOU TO COME TO ME. I CAN CHANGE YOU. I CAN MAKE YOU OVER. I CAN TEACH YOU TO BE LOVING! COME TO ME! COME TO ICARUS. . . .

"He sounds so *happy!*" I said, with disbelief and a growing panic.

"I think they call it *delirium,*" Hortense corrected. "We've got to find him before anyone else and get him out of here."

127

COME TO ME IN THE AUDITORIUM. I'M IN THE AUDITORIUM WAITING FOR ALL OF YOU. I'M WAITING.

I practically yanked Hortense's arm off as I pulled her into an exit.

"He's got the dynamite!" Hortense yelled at me. "I just know it!"

YES, ALL OF YOU COME! I'M ON THE STAGE. I'M WAITING! COME TO ICARUS, ALL OF YOU! COME TO GOD.

This time when we reached the first floor it looked like the running of the bulls in Pamplona! Lurie Bonza, Jackie Carton, and June Peckernaw were pushing and shoving along with her best pals from the cheerleading squad, including Janet Deas and Debra Kazinski. They were using Jason on the PA system as the excuse to let out shrieks like *they* were truly mad—screams to send the other kids into even greater frenzies as the whole mob galloped around the final bend near Room 101 and the main bulletin board. In another hundred feet, half of Hormone High would be hitting the auditorium at almost the same moment, so I knew something would have to give. Hortense and I managed to beat Rocky Funicelli and the other football apes. They all looked like they were part of a lynching party, a posse galloping forward to catch and kill some thief. Miss Klag stood helplessly in one doorway asking the kids to please stop, but her voice was too fragile and nobody listened to her. When Hortense and I had gotten around the bend at the bulletin board, we could see the backs of the heads of Mr. Rickenbacker and Dean Niboff and several other teachers trying to control the crazed gang storming the rear entrance of the auditorium. Helen Fitzbugh was simply jumping up and down in the air to get a better look, and Joey Masterson had climbed up on the late-pass desk. The whole school was ramming itself through the six nar-

128

row doors of the auditorium entrance, and the cranky Mr. Barrow almost knocked Hortense and me over. By the time we got into the auditorium, it was half full with screaming kids, and a handful of faculty led by Dean Niboff was standing at the bottom of the three steps that lead up onto the right side of the stage. And there was Jason! Jason Rohr standing at the top of the stairs, the wire-mesh cage of the audio system broken open behind him, clutching a microphone in his left hand.

In his right hand he held a piece of wood, a two-by-four I had seen at the construction site—but now it was a club held high keeping everyone from getting near him!

19

Hortense and I slowly pushed our way down to the near front part of the screaming crowd. The kids loved watching Jason holding off Dean Niboff, Principal Greenburg, and several of the biggest gym teachers—while he demanded to finish all he had to say. When Dean Niboff realized Jason would really whack him with the two-by-four, he signaled the teachers to stay back. Finally, the mass of Hormone High kids got tired of making these WOOOOOOOOOOOOO! WOOOOOOOOOOOOOOOOO! sounds, and even their giggles and tee-heeing disappeared. The hysteria just faded, and now everybody wanted to hear what the loony kid who thought he was a god was going to say.

With the crowd and teachers paying close attention, Jason lowered his club and spoke into the microphone in a calm, amazingly controlled voice. Then I saw Hortense slip her letter out of her pocketbook, and we inched our way down closer, hoping Jason would see us. I knew Hortense wanted to give him the letter more than anything—no matter what happened.

THE GODS ON MOUNT OLYMPUS ALWAYS SAID YOU LIVE NOT AS LONG AS YOUR BODY, Jason began, BUT ONLY AS LONG AS YOUR NAME. OUR NAMES DON'T MEAN VERY MUCH TO US ANYMORE, ESPECIALLY HERE! ESPECIALLY NOW!! BUT CHANGES HAVE TO BE MADE TODAY! THEY HAVE TO BE MADE NOW.

"You tell 'em, god!" June Peckernaw screamed suddenly like a banshee, and a mob of other kids let out jeers. But they went silent again under Jason's stare. He looked like he was truly from another planet as he stood, his limbs flung outward like the points of a star. His eyes appeared to shoot rays of light down from the stage at the thousand kids now crushed into the assembly.

EVEN IF YOU SEE ONLY A PART OF WHAT I STAND FOR, I WILL NOT HAVE LIVED IN VAIN. BUT I TELL YOU, THERE ARE POWERFUL THINGS INSIDE YOU THAT YOU'VE FORGOTTEN. THE SYMBOLS!! THE INSTINCTS! THE ARCHETYPAL FORCES! THEY'RE INSIDE ALL OF US, WAITING JUST AS I HAVE BEEN WAITING. WE NEED THEM NOW!!

Hortense took my hand and began to guide me still farther forward, closer to the stage. In her other hand she held tightly on to the letter, knowing the crowd could go berserk at any moment. I knew the closer to the stage we could get, the more we might be able to help Jason, but I also remembered that a crowd of kids can crush you to death like they do at all those South American polo games and Guadalajara rock concerts.

Dean Niboff kept giving little hand signals to staff at the rear of the auditorium, and Jason again held his club ready to discourage their approach.

WE NEED TO BUILD NEW CHILDREN. WE NEED TO DRESS THEM

131

IN THE SKINS OF LOVE AND WISDOM, Jason continued into the mike.

His voice was beginning to crack, to weaken.

WE ARE FRIENDS. I AM YOUR FRIEND.

Now he appeared to be looking directly at me and Hortense, but there was a stir from the rear of the auditorium, and Jason began to slump with what had to be pure exhaustion. We turned to look behind us and saw a half dozen police with billy clubs and gunbelts pushing their way along the left side wall, heading for the stage. The horde of kids began to scream at the sight of them, and Dean Niboff yelled from the front—that it was the lone boy on the stage they had to subdue. Hortense pulled me along faster, more urgently now, yanking me to the left of Niboff and the gym teachers and into the band pit, which still had the shining steel music stands from the morning assembly. June Peckernaw and the football team started chanting: "Icarus—Icarus—Rah Rah Rah!" and the other kids howled like wolves. The crowd parted, and as the police got closer to the front, Hortense fought more desperately to reach up toward Jason, waving the letter in her hand. It just seemed so feeble, so useless.

"Don't hurt him!" Hortense began to scream at Dean Niboff and the others waiting to help the police. "Don't hurt him!"

"Jason!" I called out helplessly.

The screaming of the kids was now deafening, the sounds of some horrible ritual; Hormone High had been transformed into some ancient arena. In a moment the police were charging up the stairs at Jason, and the kids were hissing and booing. Jason saw us, began to swing his piece of wood. Just as the cops were about to grab him, he

132

screamed in anguish, threw down the mike, and leaped out over us, grabbing the letter from Hortense's hand.

The kids on the left side of the band pit shrieked, thinking he was attacking them, but he was simply fleeing. He moved like a swift and beautiful gazelle, leaping, jumping on top of a long grand piano. In a final moment he flew through the air to the right side exit. He shoved the metal bar handle on the door, the portal flew open, and the god of Hormone High was gone.

20

By the time we made it outside along with a couple of hundred other kids, and a sprinkling of cops and teachers, it was clear Jason had miraculously escaped. Before the police even got moving in their patrol cars, we had seen him disappear at the very far end of the school's playing field, which is about a good quarter mile from the end of the building and this entire cement paddleball area where most of the kids go to eat lunch outside when the weather gets warm around May. From the point where Jason disappeared, he could have taken so many different directions, we really believed nobody would catch him. There were dozens of different weaving streets and fences, a train yard, even a couple of huge shipyards right on the river near the Bayonne Bridge, which arched from the shore high into the sky connecting Staten Island with Bayonne, New Jersey. Nobody at Hormone High could ever look at the Bayonne Bridge without remembering or hearing about the time one of our most intellectual English teachers tried to jump off it, but Dean Niboff had followed her and pulled her off the railing just in time. That was the only nice thing I had ever heard about Dean Niboff.

The rest of the day was spent calling Aunt Mo' and trying to find Jason, but nobody had seen him anywhere. Hortense and I even made two trips to see if Aunt Mo' was telling the truth, but we just knew she trusted us, and was truly very glad we were checking on Jason. But she seemed even more worried about Darwin and asked us about him.

Darwin!

Darwin. Everything had gotten so crazy we had never thought about checking with Casa de Pets. By the time we called, Dr. Montez had left for the day; but one of the orderlies got on the phone and told us Darwin was ready to go home. We were hoping he'd be in pretty good shape after a few more days of rest and vitamins at Casa de Pets. But the orderly surprised us.

"Ever since that nice blond boy stopped by, Darwin's been pacing to get out of here," he told us. "Dr. Montez said he's never seen such a recovery by a dog in his life."

"A blond boy stopped by?" I said into the phone with some amazement. Hortense's eyes were glued on me, and she shoved her head smack next to mine so we could both hear the orderly's voice on the receiver.

"Yes," the orderly said. "He said he was a friend of yours, and he sat in Darwin's cage with him for over an hour. It was the weirdest request we've ever had, but Dr. Montez said it was okay when he saw how the dog perked up at the sight of him."

"He didn't want to take Darwin with him?" I asked.

"Of course not," the orderly said, a bit confused. "The dog belongs to the girl, doesn't he?"

"Yes," I said, "sort of. . . ."

"Well, she can pick him up anytime after twelve noon tomorrow," the orderly said proudly. Then he added, with concern, "We didn't do anything wrong letting that boy see the dog, did we? He did seem a little strange, but the dog was so thrilled to see him, we assumed it was all right."

"Yes, it was all right," I said, and hung up.

When we told Aunt Mo' what had happened, even *she* was confused. We all knew Jason wouldn't let a little thing like a huge veterinarian's bill stop him from talking his way right out the door of Casa de Pets with Darwin in tow. It just seemed very clear that Jason had visited Darwin and for some reason decided to leave his pal there. But why?

By the time Hortense went home that night, I had laid a whole guilt trip on her, that Jason was probably somewhere very alone just reading her letter over and over and wanting to kill himself. She waited by the phone, but all she could think about was this terrible thing I told her about how there's always some girl or lady who ends up being a temptress to a hero and causing him a lot of pain. I'd said that she shouldn't feel bad in exactly the kind of tone which *would* make her feel awful—that whenever a hero finds his ideals aren't working out, there's always some girl around he can blame. I said the letter she insisted on writing Jason was exactly the kind of thing that would remind a hero that he wasn't a god or demigod, but only made of flesh and blood like everyone else—and Hortense got insulted. And the only thing we could figure out about why he hadn't taken Darwin out of Casa de Pets was that whatever Jason was going to do next was something he had to do alone.

A bit after the ten-o'clock news I called to apologize to

Hortense. Neither of us had heard from Jason yet, which really had us worried.

"He's going to do something dangerous," Hortense kept repeating. "That's why he didn't take Darwin!"

I kept trying to think what I would do if I ever really got into trouble, and I kept coming back to the feeling that I would talk my biggest problems out with my father. My father and I get along fine, and I know Jason would have been lucky to have a dad half as good as mine. Somehow, I just felt wherever Jason was, his thoughts were turning to his dream of having a loving father. Jason was somewhere alone, I really believed, with his mind flying backward in time and space to the invented love and guidance of Daedalus.

Anyway, neither Hortense nor I got to sleep that night—and it wasn't until the next morning when we got near Hormone High that we found out where Jason was. We had gotten off the bus and there was a tremendous crowd of people, starting from about a block before the school. Police were all over the place, and assorted other people including a couple of nuns and a priest. Dean Niboff, nearly all the teachers, and a bevy of police were flocking around the front of the big iron gate that surrounds Hormone High, and there were already several hundred kids who were being held back a good distance from the tall school fence. On the front door of the school was a big piece of oaktag with large black Magic Marker lettering:

No school today!
I have a lot of
DYNAmite...

and am going to blow it up!!! Sincerely, ICARUS!!!

And taped right above the sign was an actual stick of dynamite that Jason had put there as proof that he really had more!

Hortense gasped.

We went running down Vinnis Street past the first wooden horse, but a policeman with a huge belly blew a whistle and made us stop.

"Go back!" he yelled, coming right for us.

"We're friends of his. Where is he?"

The cop took a close look at us.

"On the roof," he said in a suddenly rather compassionate voice. "The kid's on the roof."

I looked up to the very high top of the building. Everybody was just sort of standing lined up behind the police barricade. I mean, they were all there: Miss Van der Knapp and Mr. Rickenbacker. And all of just the worst kids of Hormone High were right at the front of the barricades, including Rocky Funicelli and June Peckernaw. Most of the faculty stood really way off to the left far down Vinnis Street. And just everybody had their mouth open and their eyes glued to the top of the school.

The cop started leading Hortense and me back behind

the barricades when the voice came down from above.

"I'M GOING TO BLOW IT UP NOW! TWO MINUTES! YOU'VE ALL GOT TWO MINUTES TO GET AWAY!"

We turned, and there was Jason with no shirt and torn trousers high above the street talking into the bullhorn we had seen at his shack at the construction site.

"Jason!" we yelled, but he didn't even look down. He stepped back away from the edge of the roof and out of our sight. Dean Niboff and the cops had moved farther back just in case the entire front of the building was going to blow out. But what was really strange was the silence amongst the kids. There was no *WOOOOOOOOOO! WOOOOOOOOOOOOOOOO*ing or jeering or any of that stuff. The only sound was some honcho policeman with a bullhorn of his own—in the middle of the street talking up to the empty ridge of the roof. He was calling Jason by name, telling him this was not the way to do things, that if he had any complaints about the school, Dean Niboff was willing to sit down and discuss them. And then even the cop on the bullhorn went silent and everybody knew that *the two minutes were nearly up.* Hortense and I just stood back not knowing what to do. We thought it could be just one more way Jason was going to get attention, that he really wasn't going to blow up anything. We expected at any moment he'd come back to the edge of the roof and throw down a bunch of bulletins and that would be all. By now even the local newspaper reporter had shown up and was setting up his camera.

And then the silence ended.

It didn't suddenly end, but what happened was the huge mob of us stood gaping up and we all could hear what sounded like a small engine starting up. It was the sound of a leaf blower or a hedge clipper—perhaps more like a

139

lawn mower. It was just so weird. Nearly a couple of thousand kids and teachers and other people had collected by now, and there was only the sound of this little engine that seemed to be coming from up on the roof.

And then we began to see it.

The entire mob seemed to stop breathing. At first it appeared as though for a split second a rather large sea gull was flying from the roof, but this first glimpse of white feathers grew longer and longer and the sound of the lawnmower engine became more direct, no longer muffled by the confines of the roof. And then the entire crowd gasped at once as it saw the huge white bird, its colossal feathered wings dazzling against the sky as it left the rooftop. The shock was so great and the sight so astounding, it took many seconds before anyone could see what the contraption really was. Hortense and I knew because we had seen the hang glider in Aunt Mo's garage, but now he had really finished putting all the feathers on and affixing what looked like a lawn chair with a lawn mower driving a propeller. It just looked so freaky that even the cops and Dean Niboff were stunned. But nobody had to be stunned very long, because just as it became clear that it was Jason sitting in the chair beneath the shimmering wings, it also became clear that he and his flying machine were gaining altitude and not going to fall. Everyone looked stark raving hypnotized straight up until the next moment, when there was a tremendous *BOOOOOOOOOM!* Jason was barely a hundred feet in flight from the roof when the explosion hit. It wasn't one of those giant explosions where they use a million tons of dynamite to demolish a condemned huge hotel building or something, but it was a great blasting of one very special part of Hormone High. The entire front wall and windows of the main office and record room

140

crumbled in a tremendous *KA-BOOM,* bricks and glass shattered, and in a massive flash of fire and smoke what looked like a thousand record cabinets coughed their contents straight out as far as the end of the school fence. The front lawn of the school was a mass of burning record cards and syllabi and stockroom supplies and what looked like old curricula.

Now the crowd of kids screamed, like children at a circus where a man finally gets shot out of a cannon. They ran out onto the street, yelling and racing after the now high-flying great white bird who was Jason. Hortense and I were almost crushed to death by the stampede, and we were nearly paralyzed by fear for Jason. I wish I could say that even for a moment he looked down and saw us. I wish I could have seen him at least wave, or that we could have glimpsed a smile or a flicker of forgiveness on his face. But all he did was fly onward toward the river with the mob of kids running below as he went higher and higher. Hortense couldn't look at me as we both began to walk slowly after the crowd. We couldn't look at each other as the white wings grew smaller and farther away far above the drydocks.

We heard the police sirens. We had to move onto the sidewalk as patrol cars raced down several streets with their sirens screaming. I remember feeling chills, because by now it had sunk into my mind that the screaming mob of kids chasing the bird down past the football field and onward to the river—that their screams were more of a true cheer. It could be called an *exultation.* It was as though for the first time we were hearing anyone at Hormone High express something real and good and truthful.

"He'll make it to Bayonne. He'll get away," I said to Hortense.

She couldn't answer me. She just kept her eyes on the boy with the magnificent flying wings as he rose higher still, now above the center of the river. But he was drifting now. Jason and his contraption were drifting in the river winds and the gusts from the near, wide harbor.

"Something's wrong," I finally said, and I could feel my throat tightening.

Jason was now a speck, but his wings still shone in the sunlight as the winds swept him closer to the great arch of the bridge. We could see the winds were getting too strong for the silly lawn-mower engine and its small propeller. Even at such a distance, we could see the erratic changes of flight, the wings turning what seemed too far left and then too suddenly back to the right. The whole thing looked like it might go into a spin or at least a stall—and it looked like it was beginning to lose altitude.

We started to run, thinking if we were closer we could help. But then the end came fast. The contraption was hit by sudden and stronger winds, and before I could even yell it was blown quickly, uncontrollably into the archway of the bridge. The wings appeared to be torn in the web of cables, and pieces of white fell downward. For a moment I dreamed Jason would manage to hold on to one of the cables, that there would be a miracle, a last show of magic. Instead, the main body of the machine began to plunge downward, a hundred, a hundred and fifty feet, and it hit the sidings of the bridge roadway, almost bouncing before our friend and his dream fell the still greater distance down to the waiting deep, dark river.

21

Jason Rohr had the most unusual wake and funeral of any kid who ever passed away while attending Hormone High, and certainly the most unusual of any kid Hortense and I had ever heard of anywhere. Over seventeen hundred showed up to pay their respects during the three-day wake at Paliggini's Funeral Parlor. Almost all the Hormone High kids and at least half the faculty filed by Jason's open coffin and signed a guest book, which was really one of Jason's own looseleafs. So many showing up would have thrilled Jason.

He was laid out in one of my best suits—which I never wore anyway—and he looked like he was only sleeping except there was a clean white bandage around a part of his head. Of course, it was very strange to see a body with a bandaged head, but the rest of his face with his dark eyebrows, and some of his blond hair fanned out on a white satin pillow, all made him look very lifelike—as though he might just pop up at any moment and start giving a speech or passing out his latest bulletin. Hortense and I had cashed in our grammar-school-graduation bonds to pay Dr. Montez's bill at Casa de Pets and gotten Darwin back to Aunt Mo'. What was left we gave Aunt Mo' toward the funeral. Even the faculty took up a collection with the Hormone High kids to help Aunt Mo' pay for a very respectable funeral.

But there were only six of us and a dog at the actual burial in Wood Knoll Cemetery—the Funeral Director, a minister, Hortense, me, Aunt Mo', the mother of the girl with the big head, and Darwin at the freshly dug grave. Wood Knoll Cemetery is very close to the part of town where Hortense and I live, and since Aunt Mo's neighbor—the mother of the girl with the big head—had offered to drive Aunt Mo' and Darwin, we decided to just walk and meet everyone at the grave.

The Funeral Director was a very old man, and the minister kept it short and sweet. He was due at a christening right after, so he got to the "ashes to ashes, dust to dust" part like he was driving in the Grand Prix of Departures. Hortense hung her head so low during the whole thing, her hair fell forward hiding practically her whole profile. Naturally, I didn't show any of my real feelings, because the only way I *really* do that is when I write. I mean, it all happened so fast. I had barely time to see past my own shock, to begin focusing in on all the huge monuments and tombs and things nearby in the richer section of the cemetery—when the minister was shaking hands good-bye with everyone and offering final condolences—and Mr. Horton, the Funeral Director, signaled two grave diggers to come out from behind a giant rhododendron bush. Hortense and I hadn't even noticed those two, mainly because they looked like large primates and had blended very well into the greenery. They loped over to the coffin and began turning the cranks to lower it down into the earth. It was then that Jason's dog began to wail—a low, sad sound that made it very clear to Hortense and me that the beautiful big mutt really knew what was going on. And I wish I could tell you that something breathtakingly dramatic happened at this point, but it didn't. Jason was put in the ground and Darwin's sounds became so low and sad, they almost broke my heart.

Mr. Horton, of course, didn't just let us all stand around while the grave diggers threw dirt onto the coffin. We were directed to clear out, and he took Aunt Mo's arm and started leading her away along with the mother of the girl with the big head. For just a moment Aunt Mo' broke loose to grab the first handful of earth and sprinkle it on top of Jason's coffin—then she let herself be taken onward to her neighbor's car, which was a very old blue rusted Chevrolet. All Hortense and I could do was walk along with Darwin and Aunt Mo' and help everybody get into the car. Mr. Horton had driven his Cadillac hearse, so he got back in that and he beat everybody out of there. He had started the engine and peeled rubber out the dirt road of the cemetery. Hortense and I stayed and chatted with Aunt Mo' a few moments, telling her we'd definitely stop over to see her and Darwin and her other dogs once in a while.

"Call us if you need us," I told her.

"Are you sure you're all right?" Hortense asked her gently.

Aunt Mo' nodded she was fine, but I could see she was a lot like me and not going to show her deepest feelings.

"Ya wanna lift back?" the mother of the girl with the big head asked kindly, hunched over the front wheel.

"No, thank you," we told her. "We'll walk. We need the exercise. Thank you again."

It wasn't until they had driven practically all the way down to the main cemetery gate that Aunt Mo' turned back to look in our direction. Then I saw her hug Darwin, her face all contorted into a weeping expression like I've only seen on certain versions of the famous Mask of Tragedy you see all the time on theater programs and things like that. Anyway, that left just me and Hortense and the grave diggers inside the cemetery, and Hortense still clearly didn't feel like talking about anything, so we sat on a cement bench near a small tomb that had WEBSTER FAMILY engraved on the archway. And Hortense again dropped her head down so her hair almost hid her face, so I just watched the grave diggers filling up the rest of Jason's grave. They were far enough so I didn't have to focus in on them, and I had no idea two guys could refill a hole that size so fast without a machine or something. Actually, to be truthful, all that was really going on in my mind during that whole part on the bench was this quote Mr. Olsen had told me about by this relatively famous writer by the name of Rudyard Kipling. He would sort of tell it to anybody on the *Bird's Eye Gazette* who was in need of a little guidance on how to really write a story—or how to live a life for that matter.

> I keep six honest serving men
> (They taught me all I knew);
> Their names are What and Why and When
> And How and Where and Who.

146

Anyway, when the grave diggers had finished covering Jason's coffin and shovel pounding this big mound of dirt on the very top, I found my mind had drifted back to the story of the frog and the princess who had dragged down beneath the lake when she had broken her promise.

"Come back," the frog had called after her. "You said you'd let me be your friend!"

Something terribly important is missing was what I felt as the grave diggers packed up all their stuff and drove off in this really decrepit-looking truck. With them gone it was only me and Hortense left in the entire cemetery. At least we were the only ones who were still breathing, and I began to wonder even about that. Even with Hortense sitting right next to me, I was beginning to feel very much alone. But then, as soon as I *felt* alone, Hortense reached over and took my hand. It was really amazing to me, but since I've known Hortense, every time I've been in trouble, she's come through for me—and me for her, for that matter— when we really needed each other. I mean, we still sat on the cold cement bench in front of the tomb, but at least we were together.

"You think I killed Jason, don't you?" Hortense finally asked quietly, still not looking at me.

"No, I don't think that. . . ."

"I killed him writing those things in that letter. . . ."

"We both just wanted to be friends to him" was all I could say.

Now we were *both* looking down at the ground, but I could tell Hortense was really thinking about me. I knew she was watching me out of the corner of her eye, but I had no way of showing or telling her just then what was going on inside of me. We both just sat very still holding

147

hands and very much aware of the mound of fresh dirt across the way where Jason was.

"There's a part missing," I finally said softly.

"What do you mean?" Hortense asked.

"I mean there's something about what happened to Jason I don't understand. Something that makes me want to not believe in anything anymore."

"What do you think is missing?"

"The 'boon.' "

"The what?" Hortense asked in a soft exhale.

"There was no boon. . . ."

"What is a boon?"

"A boon is like a prize," I told her. "It's something the hero wins and brings back so the rest of the world can be better. That should have been the whole reason Jason went on his Quest—the reason any hero goes on a great adventure. It's supposed to be all right if the hero dies, but he's supposed to have returned from his quest with some kind of elixir for society or somebody. He's supposed to have brought something back that makes the whole sacrifice worthwhile. . . ."

I knew I wasn't exactly making sense, but Hortense and I had lifted our eyes and were at least looking at each other now. It was the first moment I had had a really good chance to see she wasn't wearing a whole lot of makeup on her eyes for a change. I knew we both had enough tears in our eyes so it looked like we were seeing each other underwater or through a heavy, sad mist—but in another way I was looking deeper into her eyes than I had ever done before. What Hortense looked to me most at that moment was smart. She looked damn *smart* and *deep*. And if she was looking at me with friendship and love at the same time, well—those had a chance only of running third. It was as if the same thoughts were flowing between our brains, and we would need no words. I wanted to tell her that at that moment I was seeing and feeling the secret of what seemed to me to be Life Itself. I mean, it dawned on me at that very instant that we were probably all born to be heroes— even the worst of the kids at Hormone High. That's what Jason had been saying all along. I just had this crazy idea that every kid and mother and father and assistant custodial engineer and teacher and cafeteria worker was born to hear an important Call, but most got lost along the way. We were all meant to be heroes and heroines, but nearly all have forgotten about it. Then I had to know something from Hortense.

"What would have happened to Jason if he hadn't read about the myth of Daedalus—if he hadn't become Icarus?"

"Then he might have been *no one at all,*" Hortense answered. "He might have had no identity and been trapped into some terrible darkness and silence of his mind— so alone and speechless, nothing from the outside world could ever have touched him. . . ." She looked away from me back across the rows of stones and marble slabs.

The sound of a jet flying high over us made us both look skyward. We just sat outside the tomb watching the sun sparkle on the metal form roaring above.

"Maybe *we* can be Jason's boon," Hortense said quietly, no longer able to hold back tears. "You with your writing. And me helping kids like Jason. If we always remember what he was trying to show us . . ."

I didn't answer.

"Maybe that's how he always knew it would work out," Hortense went on, "why he said you were Euripides and I was the Delphic Oracle. . . ."

I still said nothing. I couldn't speak because my brain

149

had begun to fly. What Hortense had said was sending my mind far up into the sky, higher and higher, right into the jet plane itself. In my mind I was inside its great aluminum fuselage and sitting at a window seat. I was sitting *inside the jet* with Hortense next to me, and we were both peering out the window at the colossal engines as we shot across the sky like a comet above Staten Island. And we were in the Future, looking down at our old hometown, flying over Jason's old, old grave and the graves of our parents and the graves of our teachers and even of Dean Niboff. There in the future I knew it was Hortense and I flying somewhere because we had heard a call to an important adventure— and *accepted*! Hortense and I were like Jason. Because of him we, too, had risen from ancient magic and we would go forth with amulets against all dragon forces. Hortense and I would always hear the Call to Adventure and *we would go!*

"We *will* be all he wanted us to be," I vowed.

"Yes," Hortense agreed.

Then, as the plane disappeared into a far towering cloud, we got up from the bench and began to walk—past the monuments and tombs of weathered marble, the sculptured urns and frozen shining angels—past our friend and down the winding dirt road that would take us out of the cemetery.

"Good-bye, Jason," we whispered, and then walked on.

—With melting wax and loosened strings
Sank hapless Icarus on unfaithful wings;
Headlong he rushed through the affrighted air,
With limbs distorted and disheveled hair;
His scattered plumage danced upon the wave,
And sorrowing Nereids decked his watery grave;

O'er his pale course their pearly sea-flowers shed,
And strewed with crimson moss his marble bed;
Struck in their coral towers the passing bell,
And wide in ocean tolled his echoing knell.*

*from *The Death of Icarus*, written by the very famous ancient poet Erasmus Darwin, not a dog.

THE END

DATE DUE

OCT 29 1986		
5/7/87		
SEP 26 1988		
OCT 27 1988		
MAY 09 1990		
MAY 22 1990		
SE 24 '91		
OCT 7 1991		
OCT 29 1991		
JAN 29 1992		
FEB 11 ??		
FEB 28 1992		
MAR 16 1992		
APR 01 1992		

C1   9043